VACATIONS FROM HELL

VACATIONS FROM

LIBBA BRAY

CASSANDRA CLARE

CLAUDIA GRAY

MAUREEN JOHNSON

SARAH MLYNOWSKI

HARPER TEEN

An Imprint of HarperCollinsPublishers

HarperTeen is an imprint of HarperCollins Publishers.

www.harperteen.com

Library of Congress Cataloging-in-Publication Data

Vacations from hell / Libba Bray . . . [et al.]. — 1st ed.

   v.   cm.

Summary: Five short stories in which a vacation takes a supernatural turn.

Contents: Cruisin' / Sarah Mlynowski — I don't like your girlfriend / Claudia Gray —
The law of suspects / Maureen Johnson — The mirror house / Cassandra Clare — Nowhere
is safe / Libba Bray.

ISBN 978-0-06-168873-7 (trade bdg.) — ISBN 978-0-06-168872-0 (pbk. bdg.)

1. Vacations—Juvenile fiction. 2. Supernatural—Juvenile fiction. 3. Short stories,
American. [1. Vacations—Fiction. 2. Supernatural—Fiction. 3. Short stories.]

PZ5.V246 2009   2009001408

[Fic]—dc22   CIP

                                                            AC

Typography by Amy Ryan

09 10 11 12 13   CG/RRDB   10 9 8 7 6 5 4 3 2 1

❖

First Edition

COLLEGESUMMIT.

LET TALENT SHINE

A portion of the proceeds from the sale of this collection will be donated to College Summit, a national nonprofit organization that partners with school districts to increase the college enrollment rate of all students, particularly those from low-income backgrounds.

ABOUT COLLEGE ACCESS IN AMERICA

- Every year, 200,000 students who have the ability to go to college do not enroll.
- Low-income students who get As on standardized tests go to college at the same rate as the top-income students who get Ds.

WHAT COLLEGE SUMMIT IS DOING
TO HELP SEND MORE STUDENTS TO COLLEGE

College Summit believes that sending one young person to college improves his or her life; sending a group of young people to college can improve a community; but making the college-going process work for all young people can transform our nation.

Since 1993, College Summit has reached more than 35,000 students and trained more than 700 high school teachers in college application management. Additionally, 79% of high school juniors who attend a College Summit workshop enroll in college, nearly double the national average of 46% for low-income high school graduates—an achievement that helps these students break the cycle of poverty in their families forever.

To learn more about College Summit, and for tips on what you can do to prepare yourself for college or encourage others, visit www.collegesummit.org.

Cruisin'

SARAH MLYNOWSKI

"*S*unblock?" Liz asks me.

"Check!"

"Sun hat?"

"Check!"

"Sunglasses?"

I point to the pair perched on my head. "I'm ready. Can we go?"

"Bikini?"

"Um . . ."

"Kristin, you *are* wearing the new blue bikini we bought you last week?"

"Well . . ."

She leans across her twin bed, lifts up my shirt, and gasps. "No. You are *not* wearing that hideous brown one-piece. You are not allowed to wear anything that you bought before you met me, okay?" Liz is already clad in a tiny white bikini, if you can call what looks like two pieces of string holding up three triangles a bikini.

"But I'm going to burn," I whine.

"You will not. That's why we bought SPF 100 or whatever. Don't be a baby. Put on your new suit so we can hit the deck already."

I feel queasy—and it's not because I'm stuck in a cramped cabin on a cruise ship. Although I'm sure that's not helping.

I am excited to be here—of course I am—but I'm a little nervous. I've never been on a cruise before. What if I get seasick? The boat hasn't even left port yet and already it's kind of swaying from side to side like a slightly drunk rocking chair. What if it leans in a crazy angle and I fall off? What if it slams into an iceberg and we plummet to the bottom of the ocean?

Even the name of it—the *Cruise to Nowhere*—sounds spooky. Supposedly they call it that because we're not headed anywhere specific; we're going to float around international waters for three days and three nights and then zip back to New York. But still. It sounds ominous. If I was in charge of the marketing, I'd call it *Sea Wanderer* or *Ocean Extravaganza*, or something that doesn't scream *Dead End*.

But that's just me.

Okay, I'm not just nervous about falling off the boat.

I'm really nervous because . . . All right, I'll say it. On this trip, this *Cruise to Nowhere,* I have a goal. I am going to do it.

Yes. It's time. My *first* time.

Ack. I can't believe I'm going to do *it.*

"Are you sure about the bikini?" I ask now, self-conscious. I don't bother looking at myself in the mirror. I already know what I look like. Medium boobs, shoulder-length brown hair, not too big, not too small. Just call me Goldilocks. Average, average, average. My eyes are cool, though. I'll admit that. They're kind of green and brown and blue. Swirly.

"Kristin, if you wear that hideous one-piece there is a zero percent chance you'll pick someone up. Less than zero. Minus one."

See that's the other thing. I don't actually have a candidate in mind for the big event. First step: find guy. Second: reel him in. Third: do it.

No pressure or anything. I take a deep breath.

Except what guy will give me a second look with Liz lying on a pool chair by my side? Liz, with her white string bikini, waist-length wavy red hair, and legs that are longer than my entire body. She's the Little Mermaid come to life. I bet she'd be fine if the boat pulled a *Titanic.* She'd toss her hair and twelve guys would give up their life rafts to save her.

I unzip my bag. "All right, I'll change."

"Hurry up. I want to be there when the boat—"

Before she finishes her sentence, the floor beneath us shifts. I look out through the window and over our balcony and see the pier drifting away.

My knees are shaking. Is this what they call sea legs? Or maybe I'm just nervous about what's to come. . . .

According to the map in our room, this boat has twelve floors. Twelve floors! How crazy is that? Maybe boats aren't as bad as I thought. In fact, maybe I'll move in forever. There's a spa, a hair salon, a gym, a library, a gazillion rooms, a dozen restaurants. Four pools. What else do you need?

There's already a girl about our age on the elevator when we step on. She's blond and tiny, and her skin is flushed red, like it's just been scrubbed.

"Hi," Liz says with a big smile. "Are you going to the pool on level twelve?"

Liz talks to everyone. She has no fear. I, on the other hand, feel like I've swallowed a hundred butterflies when I have to talk to a stranger.

The girl nods. "Yup. Level twelve is supposed to be the best one. It's all outside. And I need to start tanning immediately."

"I'm pretty pale too," Liz says. "So what do you think of the ship?"

"Nice. It's my first cruise."

"Mine too," I blurt. It wouldn't hurt to be a bit more fearless.

"Are you here with your family?" Liz asks.

The girl plays with the ends of her blond ponytail. "Yeah. I'm here with my insane mother. She's already taken practically a bottle of Vicodin and passed out. She'll probably sleep through the entire four days. She was supposed to be on this cruise with her new boyfriend but he dumped her last week. Not that I blame him."

Well. That was a lot of info. Liz and I give each other a look, but then turn back to the girl. "At least you got a cruise out of it," I say.

She snorts. "Lucky me. It's a crappy time to go on a cruise. Did you guys read the *National Eagle* this week?"

Liz shakes her head dismissively. "I don't read tabloids."

Me neither. Fine, sometimes I do. "Why? What does it say?"

"Do you scare easily?" she asks.

"Yes."

"Then I probably shouldn't tell you."

The doors slide open. Ow. Majorly bright. Good

thing I have my anti-UV, anti-glare, anti-any-light-getting-through-these-suckers glasses. Must protect my best asset. I slide my sunglasses over my eyes and adjust my cute new straw hat.

We survey the scene. There's a huge rectangular sparkling pool, two kitschy thatched-roof bars, and a poolside terrace restaurant. The deck is packed with people. "How about over by the deep end?" I ask, pointing to a bunch of empty blue and white striped lounge chairs.

"Come sit with us," Liz tells the new girl.

"Thanks," she says, smiling. "If you're sure you don't mind. I'm Hailey."

We introduce ourselves as Liz swipes three pale peach beach towels from a bin and claims the empty chairs.

I dump the bag between us, open the umbrella by my chair, and spread out my towel.

"So are you guys here with your parents?" Hailey asks, hunting through her bag. She pulls out a pair of oversize sunglasses and the *National Eagle*. I can't help but wonder what the so-called story is about. Do I want to know?

"Just us," Liz says, lying back in her chair.

"Wow. Are you guys sisters?" Hailey asks.

"Kind of," Liz says.

I laugh. "In spirit at least."

"Was this a graduation present or something?"

"Exactly," Liz says.

"Lucky you."

Not yet, but I plan to be. Except what's the big scary story Hailey isn't telling? "So tell us what's in the paper about cruise ships."

"I'll tell you, but don't blame me if you can't fall asleep tonight. It says, 'Vampires Attack Cruise Ships.' Isn't that insane?"

"Yes," I say. The boat sways slightly, and my stomach clenches.

"I know, right?"

Liz snorts. "*Hello*, it's the *Eagle* people. It's worse than the *Enquirer*. It's not real."

"It could be," Hailey says.

I sit up in my seat. "Wait, what exactly does it say?"

"That people have gone missing from cruise boats in the last six months. They're blaming vampires."

"Um, do they know there's no such thing as vampires?" I ask.

"Apparently not."

I shake my head. "The *Eagle* must be having serious circulation issues."

"You never know," Liz says. "Maybe vampires *are* killing people on cruise ships. Who's to say what's real and what's not?"

I lightly kick the back of her leg. "Or maybe some

psycho robs a girl who had too many vodka tonics and then shoves her overboard before anyone notices she's missing," I say.

"Yeah, that sounds about right," Hailey says, flipping through the newspaper.

"Or Bloody Marys," Liz jokes.

"I heard that happens way more than they report. It's because of the international-waters thing. It's harder to prosecute the criminals," Hailey explains.

"Or find the bodies," Liz adds.

"Scary," I say, shivering. I wrap the end of the towel around my arms.

Hailey's eyes are wide. "I'm not walking around at night, I can promise you that."

"We'll keep the bad guys away," Liz pledges, and then flips onto her stomach.

I close my eyes. Rest time.

Ahhhh. The ocean breeze in my hair, the water roaring by, the sun glittering around me. Lovely. Perfect.

I'm just about to drift off when a shadow crosses my path.

I open one eye to see what's going on and the other one promptly pops open.

Hi there.

It's a guy. A cute guy, my age, maybe seventeen. Standing between my recently pedicured feet and the pool.

He's wearing checkered black and gray bathing trunks, has cropped blond hair, and sexy sculpted arms.

Could he be the one?

With a smooth motion he dives into the water, leaving my side without even a splash to cool me down.

Where's he going? Come back, Checker Boy, come back!

"Dive in," Liz tells me, pushing herself up on her elbows.

"What?" I ask, slightly panicked.

"You like him, don't you? He's kind of yummy-looking, huh?"

"Ick. I don't even know him!" I say.

"You like what you see, right?"

"I guess," I say.

"Then dive in."

I hesitate. What if when I dive in I swallow a couple hundred gallons of chlorinated water and then lose my bikini top?

"If you want someone, you have to go after him."

"I know, but . . ."

Hailey looks up from her paper and eyes Checker Boy in the pool now doing laps. "He *is* cute, Kristin," she says. "Go for it."

Liz smiles at me as if to say, "See, even the girl we just met thinks you should."

I sigh. She's right. I know she's right. Unlike me she knows what she's doing. Unlike me she's done this before. Many, many times.

But . . . I don't want to look like an idiot. What if he blows me off? What if he has a girlfriend? What if he has a wife? What if he has children? Okay, he looks a little young to have a wife and children, but what if—

Liz sighs. "Kristin, watch how it's done." In a fluid motion she removes her sunglasses, wrap, and iPod and dives, rippleless, into the deep end.

She surfaces like a supermodel, hair glistening and shoulders pulled back to show off her oh-so-tiny bikini top. She is directly blocking Checker Boy's path.

He swims right into her. He pulls his head back, treading water and coughing.

"So sorry," Liz purrs. "Do you need mouth-to-mouth?"

Hailey laughs.

The look on Checker Boy's face says he would love some mouth-to-mouth, thank you very much. "Sorry about that," he says. "I have to learn to look where I'm going."

"I don't know if I can accept your apology," she drawls. "You may have to buy me a drink to make it up to me."

"I'll do whatever it takes," Checker Boy says, eyes

blinking rapidly, not believing his luck. They swim toward the pool bar.

"Wow," Hailey says.

"She's a master," I respond.

"But she's not twenty-one! How can she drink?"

"She has her ways."

"She stole your guy. You should have called dibs."

I shrug. "There are other fish on the boat."

An hour later Liz sashays back to our chairs.

"What's he like?" I ask.

She runs her fingers through her damp hair. "Who, Jarred? Not bad. He offered to buy me lunch. I told him we'd catch up with him later maybe."

"Does he have any cute friends?" Hailey asks.

"I didn't ask, but this one's our priority this weekend," Liz says, pointing to me. "She needs to take care of a problem."

"What kind of problem?"

My face heats up, and it's not from the sun.

"Her virginity," Liz says with a half smile.

"Oh, don't do it," Hailey says. "I wish I would have waited. I lost it last fall, beginning of junior year, to a total idiot. He told the entire school."

"Jerk," I say.

"So trust me, don't rush," she says. "Wait for someone

you're madly in love with."

"Do not listen to her," Liz says. "It will be too scary to do it with someone you're madly in love with."

"Maybe," Hailey says, hesitating. "At least if you do it with some random stranger, it won't matter who he tells. It's not like you'll know the same people. Have you ever come close to losing it?"

"Once," I admit.

"What happened?"

I hesitate. "It was with a guy named Tom. I thought it was going to happen. I was in his room. His parents weren't home. And I was just about to when . . ."

"When what?"

"I chickened out," I admit. "And bolted."

"He must have loved that." Hailey laughs.

"I'm sure he got over it," I say. Not that I ever saw him again. Better off for both of us, I'd say.

"What about you?" Hailey asks Liz. "When did you lose it?"

She shakes her head. "It feels like forever ago." She shrugs. "Who can remember?"

Hailey stretches her arms above her head. "I should probably go check on my mom. Make sure she hasn't thrown herself off the side of the boat."

"Or gotten attacked by vampires," Liz says, winking.

Hailey laughs. "Will you guys be around later?"

"Yup," I say.

"Cool."

"We'll be at the casino," Liz says, reclining in her seat again. "Meet us at nine."

"Great. Thanks."

"Wait, Hailey?" I ask. "Are you finished with the *Eagle*?"

"Yup. You want it?"

"Yeah, if you don't mind."

She tosses it on my chair. "Enjoy."

Liz snickers as I open the paper.

"It's not funny," I say, reading the details. "It says there have been *seven* disappearances on six different cruise ships in the past year. Two people were found in the water, drained of blood. Drained of blood! Aren't you even a little bit worried?"

"Gimme a break. It's the *Eagle*. Hello, there's no such thing as vampires, remember? Anyway, you're transferring your anxiety from what you're really afraid of."

"And what's that?"

She gives me a knowing look. "You know. Losing it."

"Thank you, Dr. Laura. But I don't want to talk about it anymore." I flip over in my lounge chair, turning my back to her.

"Are you hungry?" she asks a few minutes later.

"No," I say, still mad.

"Stop being a baby," she says. "I'm starving. I'll get us something to eat. Let me find Jarred."

"Hailey says I should have called dibs."

"Hey, he's all yours if you want him," she offers.

"No, you go ahead. I don't want your charity. I'll find my own guy." I take a deep breath of ocean air. "Promise."

Liz and I meet Hailey at the casino later that night, by a James Bond slot machine. If I put in a quarter, will a gorgeous spy pop out?

"You two look amazing," Hailey says.

"So do you," I say. She does look very pretty in a simple black cotton dress.

"Oh, please, you guys look like you're going to a Manhattan gala, and I look like I'm going to a school dance." She admires the purple strapless dress Liz forced me into and Liz's glamorous backless red sheath. "Can I come raid your closet?"

"Anytime," Liz says, fixing the strap on her shoe. "And you smell great. What perfume is that?"

Hailey smiles. "Thanks! It's called Parfum de Vie."

"Very yummy."

"How's your mom?" I ask.

"Passed out. So pathetic." She rolls her eyes and straightens her shoulders. "What do you wanna do?

Gamble? Scope the scene? Find cute boys? Slay vampires?"

"I'm up for the first two," Liz says, and scans the room. "Let's start at the bar."

When we make our way over, a much older but still very hot bartender asks us what we'd like to drink. Liz purrs her order over the bar, showing extra cleavage.

She turns back to us and murmurs, "Dibs."

"He's old enough to be your father," Hailey says.

"I like mature men. They smell better. Like fine wine." She lifts her glass to ours and we clink.

As I lower my glass, I spot him.

The one.

I know right away. He's it. He's perfect.

Standing by the blackjack table.

If I thought Checker Boy was cute, this guy is a whole other level of cute. The level twelve of cute. He's gorgeous. Tall, shiny dark hair, sculpted cheekbones, shoulders like a quarterback's. Unlike Mr. Bartender he can't be more than twenty-two. And he's wearing a tux.

Seriously.

Who needs a quarter? I just found my very own James Bond. An old-school, dark-haired one too. Go me.

"Dibs," I whisper.

Liz squeezes my shoulder. "Good call."

"I'm in love," I say.

"I can see that," she says. "Wipe your chin. You drooled."

"Where, where? Show me him!" Hailey says, jumping in place.

"Don't be too obvious," I warn her, flipping my hair in my most nonchalant way. "Look over at the blackjack table."

She oh-so-casually spins a hundred and eighty degrees. "Ooooh. He's hot. Go for him!"

I fidget with my dress. "How? What do I do?"

Hailey turns to Liz. "Yeah, tell us what to do. How did you know what to do to get that swimmer at the pool? Where is he anyway? Are you meeting up with him?"

Liz shrugs. "Nah. It's over. He was boring."

Hailey laughs. "I guess you already found someone new. Tell us your secrets so we can follow in your footsteps, will you?

She motions us closer. "It's all about the attitude. He should know that you think you're all that. If you think you're all that, he'll think you're all that. But being all that doesn't mean 'I'm better than you.' It means, 'I'm fantabulous and you seem like you are too, so maybe we deserve each other.'"

"Fantabulous?" I repeat.

"Yes." She nods emphatically. "Absolutely fantabulous."

"I can do that," Hailey says. "I can be absolutely fantabulous. What else?"

"That's it."

"That's all it takes to find a boyfriend?" Hailey asks.

Liz grins. "Boyfriend? Who wants a boyfriend? That was how to score a hook-up." She rubs my shoulders again. "So are you ready?"

"Yes," I say while shaking my head no.

"Go play next to him. There's a seat open."

"But I don't know how," I whimper.

She tosses me a black chip. "Aim for twenty-one."

"Er, twenty-one what?"

When she laughs, I take a deep breath and head over to the empty stool. *I can do this.* "This seat taken?" I ask in an unfortunately nasal voice.

He tilts his head to the side and gives me a blinding smile. "Nope. All yours."

I gingerly place one chip on the felt table.

"Having a good night?" I ask, attempting to sound a wee bit more sophisticated and seductive. In other words I sound like I have strep.

"Yeah. My friend just got married in the dining room," he says. "I was all danced out, so I snuck in here for a break."

That explains the tux. "Fantabulous," I say.

"Sorry?"

"Oh, um . . . happy wedding. You look too young to have a friend getting married."

"Oh, he's crazy. College buddy. You know how it is. What college do you go to?"

"NYU," I lie instantly. Why not? It's not like he'll ever know the difference.

He nods, buying it. "I'm at Penn. Hey," he says, leaning closer to me and putting his hand on my arm.

A jolt of static runs through my body. He's so close I can smell the aftershave on his neck.

"You have the coolest eyes," he says slowly as I watch his mouth forming the words.

"Thanks," I say, barely breathing.

The dealer interrupts us by distributing two rounds of cards to the four of us at his table.

James Bond lets go of my arm and settles back onto his seat.

Sigh.

I stare down at my cards. An eight and a jack. I have no idea what that means. I try to smile at James, but he seems to be over me and my eyes and is now enthralled by his cards.

"Miss?" the dealer asks me.

"Yes?" I ask back.

"What would you like to do?"

I look at my hand. I have no idea. "Get a card?"

Mr. Bond looks at me in shock. "What? Why?"

Too late. The dealer hands me the four of spades and declares me out.

Whoops.

Not feeling that fantabulous right now. More like moronic.

"What happened?" Liz cries when I return empty-handed in all senses of the word. No chips, no boy.

"I lost all my chips. I had no idea what I was doing!"

"Why didn't you ask him for help?"

"How does one ask for help when one is trying to appear fantabulous?"

She tosses her hair behind her shoulder. "You can still be fantabulous and not know how to play blackjack."

"Well, the dealer got an ace and a jack so apparently he won. And before—"

Liz squeezes my arm. "But what happened to the boy?"

I sigh. "He said he'd see me around and disappeared. I give up. I'm going to watch TV in bed."

Liz adjusts her dress. "I'm going to hang out with the bartender. Guess I can't take him back to our room, then."

"Sorry."

"No problem. I'll find somewhere to go."

"Avoid the deck," Hailey tells her.

Liz winks. "Don't wait up."

"She's a master," Hailey says, and gives Liz a small bow.

And I'm the worst pupil ever.

"Why isn't he here?" I wonder out loud.

Liz yawns. "Because it's nine A.M. Did we really have to get here this early? We're the only ones at the pool."

"I don't want him to disappear again."

"It's not like he has anywhere to go. He's kind of boat-locked."

"As long as a vampire doesn't get him and throw him overboard," I say, and stretch my legs out in front of me. "Hailey is meeting us around eleven."

"What do you think of her?" she asks me.

"I like her," I say. "You?"

"There's something off about her. I like it."

"Maybe she's a vampire," I say.

"She is *not* a vampire," Liz says.

"She's pale. Good sense of smell. She's traveling alone."

"She's here with her mom," Liz reminds me.

"So she says."

Liz closes her eyes and then opens them again. "I'm hungry. Wanna get something to eat?"

"Um, no thanks. I'm still full from your midnight

treat. Thanks for bringing me that snack from the bar, by the way."

"Alrighty, I'll see you later." She blows me a kiss and sashays off.

I don't mind having a minute alone. The breeze is in my hair, the sky is bright blue—it's a perfect day.

What could be better?

James. Seeing James could make this better. Yes, I know James Bond isn't his real name, but I can call him whatever I like. I sigh and close my eyes. There are lots of other guys who could be my first. But there was something about James. . . . He'd be perfect. He's the one! My first! Of course he doesn't know this yet. He doesn't even know my name yet. I don't even know his name yet. In fact I hardly know anything about him except that he's a student at Penn and he looks great in a tux.

But I know he's perfect.

I have to find him.

By eleven Hailey has set up next to me. By twelve Liz is back with messy hair and a naughty smile on her face.

"And what took you so long?" I ask.

She winks. "Wouldn't you like to know."

By two there's still no James at this pool, and I decide I might as well look around the ship. "I wonder where he is," I say.

If he's not going to come to me, I'm going to have to go to him.

"Anyone wanna come stalk James with me?" I ask.

"Definitely," Liz says, slipping on her flip-flops.

The three of us hit the deck.

"Let's see," Liz says. "There are three other pools on the boat. Which one will he be at?"

"Let's start at the top and work our way down," Hailey suggests.

We try the eleventh-floor pool first. Kiddie pool. No James.

"At least I know he has no children," I say. There you go—now I know three things about him.

We try the tenth-floor pool next. It's the fitness pool. It's long and rectangular, and there are a whole bunch of hard-core workout buffs swimming laps.

No James. No sun either, since it has a roof. I flip my sunglasses to the top of my head.

"I like this pool," Hailey says, ogling the pumped-up guys hard at work. "Can we come back here later?"

"Watching them is too tiring," Liz says. "Next!"

Last pool—ninth floor. We step out of the elevator and—

Omigod. "There he is!" I say, pointing. James! In the flesh! In the hot tub! Oh! Even though there's a roof, he's wearing aviator sunglasses, and he's holding a beer and he's just as gorgeous as I remember and he's sitting next to a girl and—

A girl. Who is this girl and why is she stalking my man? I'm the only one who gets to stalk my man.

The girl is giggling at something James is saying: a high, tinkling, annoying giggle, a giggle that makes me want to kill her.

His hand is resting on her shoulder.

"Booooo," I moan. "I think my boyfriend already has a girlfriend."

I stomp my sandaled foot against the deck.

"You're cuter," Hailey says.

Liz nods. "You can take her."

I shake my head. "I can find a single guy. I don't need to rob someone of her boyfriend."

"It's not a girlfriend," Liz says. "It's some random girl he's flirting with. I saw her last night at the casino with a whole other group. She'll be history by dinner."

"You think?" I ask hopefully.

"I promise," she says.

We all split up in the late afternoon: Hailey claims she needs a nap, Liz hits the gym, and I check out the spa. We all meet for dinner and a little YMCAing at the disco. Later we find James Bond back at the casino bar.

The good news: Liz was right—the girl from the

afternoon is nowhere to be found.

The bad news: He's with two new girls. He's smiling at both of them, his teeth gleaming against his pale skin.

Sigh.

"Next," Hailey whispers.

"But he's so perfect," I say. "Look at him."

"Kristin, you can't just hook up with someone who's already hooked up with two people in as many days," she says, shaking her head. "That's skanky. No offense, Liz."

"None taken," Liz says cheerfully.

"It's not like I want a deep, meaningful relationship," I mumble.

"But he's a creep. What happened to the girl in the hot tub? Has he forgotten all about her already?"

His arm is gently brushing against the back of one of the girls, the one in a pink halter top. The other girl, wearing her hair in a tight bun, is twirling on a bar stool, looking bored and annoyed. She whispers something to Miss Pink Halter Top and then takes off.

"Great. Now the lovebirds are on their own." I throw my hands in the air. "I give up!"

"Let's go get ice cream sundaes," Hailey suggests. "They're giving them out in the dining room. I bet there are better guys there. Ones that aren't so cocky looking."

"But I like cocky guys," I say sadly.

We step back out into the lobby. "You two go ahead," Liz says. "I have someone I need to talk to."

"Your friend from last night?" Hailey asks knowingly.

Liz winks.

We go for ice cream. Hailey takes two bowls: one for her and one for her alleged mother.

"Not that she'll eat it," Hailey says. "It'll probably just melt into a pile of gunk."

"Has she not left her room?" That is so weird. Could that even be true? How could we not have seen her at least once?

"I think she has a few times. But only at night. She sleeps all day. It's ridiculous."

"Want me to come check on her with you?" I ask. To see if she really exists. Maybe she's the vampire. Ha-ha.

"Oh no. Don't worry about it. She'd hate it if I brought someone back to the room. Wanna go to yours and hang out? I can meet you there after I drop this off. Don't you have a balcony?"

"I do, but . . ." Not a good idea. "My roomie might have a friend there. And we don't want to . . . ruin the mood."

"This is it," Liz says the next day at the pool. "Our last full day. Are you ready to make your move, sweetie?"

"I've been ready for three days." Kind of. Hopefully. I scan the pool area for his gorgeousness. "He's not even here."

"He will be," she says.

"If you really want to make it happen, I think you may need to choose someone else," Hailey says. "You're practically out of time."

"But he's my dream man," I say. "I just need to get him alone."

"And I doubt you will any time soon," Hailey says, pointing with a toe across the pool. "Look who's over there by herself."

The girl with the bun from last night, the friend of Pink Halter Top girl, is talking to one of the waiters.

"Oh great," I say.

"Her friend is probably all cuddled-up with your boy. Time for you to move on."

The girl sees us staring and hurries over.

"What could she want?" Hailey wonders aloud.

When she reaches our chairs, she says, "Hey, sorry to bother you guys. But you were at the casino last night, right?"

"Yeah," Liz says.

"Did you see me and my sister? We were talking to a guy named Jay?"

Seriously? His name is Jay? That is so close to James.

Is that not a sign that he was meant to be my first, or what?

"I saw," I say.

"Have you seen my sister since then?" she asks hopefully. "Here somewhere?"

The three of us shake our heads.

"Maybe she's still with . . . Jay?" I say. "My Jay," I want to add but don't.

The girl sighs. "Do you mind if I sit down?"

"Of course, sweetie, take a load off," Liz says, pulling in her knees to make room.

"I'm Ali," she says. "And my sister is not with Jay."

"Are you sure?" I ask hopefully.

She nods. "I went by his room this morning. She wasn't with him. I asked him where she was and he said he had no idea."

That's good news, right? "But didn't she go off with him last night?"

"He says she didn't," the girl says. "But that doesn't make sense. She never came back to the room. Her bed is still made. Where else could she be?"

Liz pats her arm. "Maybe she met some other guy?"

"I guess. . . ."

"I'm sure that's it. She probably met some guy and went back to his room."

"But that's so unlike her! I mean, she liked Jay; why would she just hook up with someone else?"

"I'm sure she's around somewhere," Liz says, continuing to pat the girl's arm. "Do you want me to help you look for her?"

"Would you? I'd really appreciate it. It's just the two of us, and I'm getting a little freaked out—"

"No worries," Liz says, tying on her wrap. "I'm happy to help."

"Do you want us to come?" I ask.

"No, you guys stay here in case . . ."

"Carly," Ali says.

"In case Carly turns up."

"Are you creeped out?" Hailey says to me as Liz and the new girl head to the elevator.

"Hmm?"

"Are you creeped out?"

"About what?" I ask, truly clueless.

She pulls her legs into a cross-legged position. "Um, the fact that her sister was with Jay last night and disappeared?"

"But Jay told her Carly wasn't with him," I say.

"Sure, he *said* that, but what if he's lying?"

I shrug. "Why would he lie?"

"He would lie if he *did* something to her!"

"Like what?"

"Like many things! Something bad! Gotten her

drunk, robbed her, or thrown her over the boat railing. He could be a killer. We don't know anything about him except that he's good-looking."

"Not true," I say. "We think that he has no children. That he enjoys female company. We know he's here for a wedding, and that he goes to Penn."

"So he says. Don't you think it's all a little weird? The girl he was with last night is missing. And . . . come to think of it, what happened to the girl from the hot tub? I haven't seen her around either." She turns white. "Omigod."

"What?"

"The story about the vampire. What if *he's* the vampire?"

I almost laugh. "Oh, come on. Jay is *not* a vampire."

"He could be."

My Jay is not a vampire. "No he *can't*."

"Yes he can! Think about it." She rubs her temples. "We only see him at night."

"Not true. We saw him in the hot tub. That was during the day."

"Oh, right." Her forehead creases. "But it was indoors! Ha! No direct sunlight."

"Uh-huh."

"You think it's a joke, but he could be dangerous. If I were you I would stay clear of him. Don't let him try to get you alone."

Let him? At this point I can't *force* him to be alone with me.

An hour later Liz is back, looking satisfied. "All good," she says, lying back down in her chair. "Sister found."

Hailey claps. "Seriously?"

"Yup." She reaches into her bag and reapplies her sunblock.

Hailey sighs. "Thank god. Where was she?"

"She got up early and went to the spa. Ali must have been sleeping when she left the room."

"But I thought her bed was made?"

Liz shrugs. "Guess she made it."

"Who makes her own bed on a cruise?" I ask.

"You'd have to ask her," Liz says with a shrug.

Or not.

The tension melts from Hailey's face. "Omigod. That is such a relief."

"Hailey was about to report Jay for being a vampire," I say, giggling.

"I was nervous!" Hailey cries.

Liz raises an eyebrow. "You think Jay is a vampire?"

"Not anymore," she says. "Although he does kind of look like a vampire. Don't you think?"

"What does a vampire look like exactly?" I ask, still giggling.

"You know. Pale skin. Dark hair. Brooding eyes."

Liz smiles. "Sounds sexy."

"Vampires *are* sexy," Hailey admits. "Brad Pitt? Sexy. Angel? Sexy. Edward? Super sexy. I would totally do it with a vampire."

Liz pokes me. "Speaking of doing it . . ."

"I know, I know."

"Tonight is your last chance," she continues. "You are going to find your vampire boyfriend and tie him down until you've done it. Enough is enough. Got it?"

"Got it," I say, pounding my fists against the lounge's handles. "Tonight is the night. No idea what I'm going to say to him but—"

"Why do you have to talk to him at all?" She wiggles her eyebrows.

"Get your mind out of the gutter." I laugh.

"Just try to get yours in the gutter, where it belongs."

"She has to say something to him," Hailey says. "She can't just start making out with him."

"I very much doubt he would mind that," Liz says.

"I don't know why you're going to waste your virginity on him anyway," Hailey says. "Sure he's cute, but he seems like a jerk. In all likelihood he hooked up with at least two other girls in three days. He doesn't sound like a catch. He sounds like a player."

Liz waves Hailey's words away. "Players are the best choices. Trust me. He's the one. You'll have a lot more fun."

I nod. I know she's right. "So what should I do?"

"Be fearless."

"Do what you want," Hailey says. "But if I were you I'd shy away from hickeys."

When I see him at the bar, I know the time is right.

This is it.

He's sitting by himself. Waiting. For me.

Okay, fine, probably not for me, but he's alone, isn't he? Good enough.

Hailey and Liz are in our room. Liz told Hailey she could borrow an outfit.

I square my shoulders and take a deep breath. I can do this. *I can do this.*

"Hi," I say, my heart pounding. "Can I buy you a drink?"

He gives me a gleaming smile. "You want to buy me a drink?"

"I offered, didn't I?"

"It must be my lucky night," he says, eyes twinkling. Omigod, he smells amazing. Musky and salty and absolutely delicious. I knew he would!

"I think it's definitely your lucky night," I say, my cheeks burning. I can't believe I just said that. I wave the bartender over. "What would you like?"

"A Bloody Mary," he says, and smiles at me.

Really? People actually drink that? Liz would laugh

out loud. Who knows, maybe it's good. "I'll have one too," I tell the bartender.

"Jay," he says, and gulps down the drink.

"Oh, I know," I say brazenly. "I mean, nice to meet you. I'm Kristin."

Crap. Should I have told him my real name? Does it really matter?

"Since it's my lucky day, maybe we should hit the tables," he says. His teeth are tinged red.

He does look a little like a vampire. Not that he is. Of course he isn't.

My heart starts pounding. Can I really do this?

"We could," I say, and lean in toward him so he can see just a little bit down the top of my shirt. Hello, fearless me. "Or maybe you want to get out of here?"

His eyes light up like candles. "Seriously?" He grins. "Yeah, I'm up for that. Wanna check out my room?"

"Do you have a roommate?" I ask, my heart thumping.

"No. But I have a balcony."

"Sounds good," I say, downing the rest of my drink for liquid courage.

He takes my hand. "Come with me."

Here we go! I did it! Okay, I didn't do it *yet*, but I am in the ready position.

We are standing on his balcony. The sky is liquid black and sprinkled with shining stars. The wind blows through my hair and makes my skin tingle. I hold on to the banister and take a deep breath of sea air.

"Nice out here, huh?" he asks.

"It's amazing."

He puts his arm around my shoulders. "So," he says.

"So," I respond. I turn back toward him. Here it is. My chance. All I have to do is not chicken out.

His face inches closer to me. And closer. I'm breathing his salty smell. I can almost taste him.

And then . . . we're kissing.

We're kissing!

Yay!

He kisses me harder. He runs his fingers through my hair. He lowers his hand to the small of my back and pulls me into him. He stops kissing me only to tell me how beautiful I am, which is so nice. *He's* so nice.

Oh my. What am I doing? Can I go through with this?

I don't know. I feel sick.

I don't think I can do this.

I can't do this.

I pull back.

"I'm sorry, James. I mean Jay. I mean . . ." I have to get out of here. "I thought I could do this. But I can't."

"Huh?" he says, startled, eyes blinking open.

"I have to go. Now. Trust me."

"But, but . . ." He grips my shoulders. "We're not done."

Excuse me?

"You can't lead me on like that and then not finish what you started," he says, his voice low and rumbly.

"I don't think that's the way it works," I tell him.

"I think it is," he says, pulling me back toward him.

"No, it really isn't. I'm not ready."

"You seem ready to me."

Maybe he's right. Maybe I am ready. I try to relax. I take a deep breath. This *is* what I want. He certainly deserves to be my first.

"Hmm," I say, taking a deep breath. I kiss the edge of his lips. And then his cheek. And then I nibble on his ear. Carefully. And then I move down to the top of his neck. He just smells so delicious. Tasty. The real Parfum de Vie—scent of life. Hungry, I kiss his neck. Lick his neck. Lick off the aftershave. Yum.

"That feels so good," he murmurs.

I open my mouth wider. Here it comes. I'm ready. I can do this. Be fearless.

I sink my teeth into his neck.

"Hey!" he screams. "That hurts." He tries to pull back.

Now it's too late to go back. It's time. I pull him back toward me, steady his face between my cold hands, and bite him again.

Liz was right. This isn't *that* hard.

As he pointlessly struggles to get away, he asks, "Why are you doing this to me?"

Because I'm thirsty, I think but don't say. I'm too busy drinking.

"What . . . are you?" he mumbles just before he passes out.

I swallow a mouthful of blood. Much better than a Bloody Mary. "I'm a vampire," I explain, and then finish him off.

I did it. I did it!

My first time. I have to admit, I'm kind of proud of myself.

Once I've drained his body, I heave it over the railing and watch him disappear into the blackness below.

After I hear a soft splash, I let myself out.

I find Hailey and Liz alone on the pool deck.

Hailey is lying across a lounge chair, her eyes wide open, her arms and legs trembling.

"Yay, you did it!" Liz says. "Full?"

"Stuffed," I say. "Extra delicious. Fantabulous. Even better than Checker Boy, or the old bartender, or hot tub girl."

"Fresh is always better than leftovers."

"You are absolutely right."

"Although you didn't taste Ali or Carly," Liz says. "They were pretty tasty."

I look down at Hailey, who's staring into the sky, still trembling. "I thought she'd be overboard by now. You decided to change her instead?"

Liz nods. "Yeah. You don't mind, do you? I like her. I think she'll be fun. I gave her the choice, of course. She said she was up for something new. She doubts her mom will even notice she's different."

Laughter wafts from the other end of the deck. We look up. Two college guys are walking over to us. One of the guys is wearing a Yankees hat.

Hailey pushes herself up on her elbows.

"You okay?" I ask.

She nods, and then, her hand no longer shaking, points to the guy in the hat and whispers, "Dibs."

*I Don't Like
Your Girlfriend*

CLAUDIA GRAY

Part One

VACATION CHECKLIST

- ✓ sundress
- ✓ sandals
- ✓ black bikini in case I am feeling brave
- ✓ purple one-piece in case I am being chicken
- ✓ stovetop autoclave
- ✓ sunglasses
- ✓ crushed clamshell
- ✓ snake venom
- ✓ moth wings
- ✓ iPod

SELF-IMPROVEMENT GOALS

This year at the Outer Banks I will:
- be nicer to Theo, who Mom swears looks up to me even if he shows it by putting dead starfish in my shoes
- review stuff with Mom alone after coven meetings so I don't forget it all before we get home
- ignore Kathleen Pruitt's bitchery because I am too good to stoop to her level

"I know you're methodical, but this is ridiculous."

Cecily Harper looked up from her notepad to see her father standing in the doorway, arms folded across his chest and a smile on his face. She underlined her last words with a theatrical flourish. "You know, making lists is one of the seven habits of highly effective people."

"Honey, I'm used to your lists," her father said. "You started making them as soon as you could spell. But your suitcase—you packed all your clothes by color."

She looked at her open suitcase on the bed. The whites were nestled at one end, the blacks at the other, with the brighter shades in between. Shrugging, Cecily said, "Well, how do *you* do it?"

Affectionately he tousled her hair. This was slightly annoying, because she'd just fixed her ponytail, but Cecily didn't worry about it for very long. She was much more worried about the fact that her father had caught sight of something unusual in her suitcase.

He picked up the vial of moth wings and frowned. "What is this?"

"Uh." Cecily tried to think of a lie, but she couldn't. "Um . . ."

His expression shifted from curiosity to disgust. "Cecily, are these—bug wings?"

Tell him the truth.

"Yes." Flushed with daring, Cecily added, "They're moth wings for magic spells."

Dad stared at her. "What?"

"Cecily, don't tease your father." Her mother stepped into Cecily's bedroom and briskly took the jar. "Simon, these are soap flakes. Bubble bath. They make them look like moth wings and eye of newt and all that sort of magical stuff now. I think it's some Harry Potter thing."

"Harry Potter." Dad chuckled. "Those merchandising guys don't miss a trick, do they?"

Mom tucked the jar back into the suitcase and shot her daughter a warning look. But her voice was cheery as she said, "Let's hurry up, guys. We should leave for the airport in about fifteen minutes. Sweetheart, would you check on Theo? The last time I saw him, he was trying to sneak Pudge into his carry-on."

"For Christ's sake." Dad started down the hall. "All we need is for the Department of Homeland Security to detain us because of the hamster."

As soon as her father was out of earshot, her mother muttered, "Do we have to have this talk again?"

"I'm really sorry I endangered all our lives." Cecily tossed her hair melodramatically, clutching her hands in front of her chest like a silent-movie heroine. "What if Dad tries to have us burned at the stake? Whatever shall we do?"

"Load your bag in the car, all right? And don't even think about pulling a stunt like that once we get to North Carolina. The others aren't going to cut you as much slack as I do."

Her mother hurried off, unbothered by the latest in their many tiffs on this subject. But Cecily felt angry with herself for making a joke of it instead of trying to talk this through.

Usually she tried hard to respect the rules of the Craft, rules Cecily had memorized before she'd turned eight years old. Most of the rules were sensible—the necessary reins on the incredible powers that they worked with. The fact that she knew those rules backward and forward was one reason that she was already a fine witch.

In Cecily's opinion there was another reason. She didn't only memorize the rules; she pushed herself to understand the reasons behind them. For instance, it was one thing to know that the Craft forbade witches to use their powers to undermine the wills of others; it was another to understand *why* that was wrong and how misusing the powers that way would corrode both your ability and your soul.

Yet there was one rule Cecily could never understand, the oldest of them all: *No man may know the truth behind the Craft.*

Dad—who knew nothing about the single most important thing in the lives of his wife and his daughter—called, "We've got to drop Pudge off at the O'Farrells and get to the airport within one hour. Unless nobody wants to go to the beach house this year!"

Cecily shook off her melancholy and zipped her suitcase shut. Time to go meet the coven.

Of course, none of the men involved knew the annual Outer Banks trips had anything to do with witchcraft. They all believed that this was a reunion of "college friends": six women who remained very close and wanted their families to know one another. So each year they rented a couple of North Carolina beach houses within walking distance of one another and split them between the families. The trips had begun before Cecily was born, so by now the six husbands were good friends too, and they liked to say that their kids were "growing up together." Cecily could happily have skipped the experience of growing up with Kathleen Pruitt.

"We have a coven at home," Cecily had complained last month when she'd asked to skip the Outer Banks for one summer. "Why can't we just spend extra time with them instead of hanging with the witches you practiced with in college? I learn more that way."

But her mother wouldn't hear of it. She insisted that some covens had a special energy that made it worthwhile to keep in touch and someday Cecily would understand. When Cecily tried to explain that a week with Kathleen Pruitt was like six months in hell, Mom had said she was being dramatic. (Mom might have understood if Cecily had told her about that stunt the year before, when Kathleen had loudly claimed on the beach that Cecily's tampon string was hanging from her swimsuit, which it *so was not*. But Cecily could never bring herself to speak of it.) So the Outer Banks. Again.

At least they were at the beach. Cecily, who loved swimming in the sunshine, thought that was every summer's silver lining.

Except, of course, if it was raining.

"The weather report swore this front would stay south of here," Dad said, turning up the windshield wipers of the rental car to top speed.

Theo kicked impatiently at the back of their mother's seat. "You said I could swim as soon as I got there. You *promised*."

"I'll bet the storm blows over soon," Mom said soothingly.

Theo would not be consoled. "We can't even use the Jacuzzi tub if it's raining!"

Cecily looked at the heavy dark clouds with foreboding. *What could be worse than spending a week with your worst enemy?* she thought. *Being trapped inside with her* and *your whiny little brother because of the rain. That's worse.*

Then she reminded herself of her goals not to worry about Kathleen Pruitt and to be nicer to Theo, who was only eight years old and couldn't be expected to have any perspective. "Hey, remember the foosball table in the front room?" She poked his shoulder. "Last year, you couldn't beat me, but you're bigger now. You should challenge me to a rematch."

"I guess that would be okay." Theo sighed, still pretending to pout. But Cecily could see the gleam of mischief in his eyes. When she threw the foosball game, he'd be thrilled.

When they reached the beach house, a couple of her mother's friends rushed out to greet them, storm or no storm. Mrs. Silverberg, Ms. Giordano—they looked so ordinary, in their mom jeans and pastel-colored polo shirts. No man alive (nor most women) would ever guess the powers they taught to their daughters. Now they shouted hellos while raindrops softened the sheets of newspaper they'd tented over their heads, and there were big hugs for everyone. Cecily tried hard to look enthusiastic, though it was difficult while she was getting drenched.

While her father grabbed most of the luggage, Cecily glanced around warily for Kathleen. One year she'd met Cecily at the car—only to hit Cecily's bag with an itching spell. Cecily's mother hadn't figured out the real problem for two whole days, during which Cecily had scratched her arms so raw that swimming in the ocean was impossible.

There was no sign of Kathleen, though. Slightly relieved, Cecily tugged the last suitcase—hers—from the trunk, grimacing at the weight and wondering if she'd really needed that autoclave. Then a strong hand reached past her to clasp the handle. "Let me get that."

Cecily glanced over her shoulder at the most gorgeous guy she'd ever seen.

He had blond hair and blue eyes, so striking that she started thinking dorky things about golden sand and dark seas. He was perhaps a foot taller than Cecily, who normally preferred guys closer to her own height but felt she would make an exception in this case. His white T-shirt was rapidly becoming transparent as it got wet, which was the best reason Cecily could think of to stay outside in the rain.

"Heavy," he said, lifting her bulging suitcase with no

apparent effort. "You must have packed a lot."

"Every year I promise myself I'll bring less," she confessed. "I never quite manage it."

He smiled even more broadly. "That means you want to be prepared for anything."

Gorgeous, polite, and *understands the value of thorough preparation. I've got to be dreaming.*

"Cecily?" Mom called from the steps of the house. "Are you two going to stand out there all day?"

"Coming!" Cecily answered. The Gorgeous Polite Guy laughed softly as he toted the bags inside.

Her sandals squished against the floor as she came into the beach house, which they were supposed to call "Ocean's Heaven." (All the houses at the Outer Banks had stupid beach-pun names, and they had driftwood sculptures on the walls and bedspreads with patterns of pelicans or seashells.) Cecily's T-shirt and cropped cargos stuck to her in weird, uncomfortable folds, and her makeup had probably all been washed into the sand. What would Gorgeous Polite Guy think? Quickly she wrung out her bedraggled ponytail and parted her dripping bangs—to see Kathleen Pruitt.

"*There* you are," Kathleen said. "I was just asking Mom where you could be. You look just the same!"

Drops of water from Cecily's soaked clothing pattered onto the rug of the beach house. "Wow, thanks."

If Kathleen noticed the sarcasm, she ignored it.

Cecily would've liked to add a snide comment about Kathleen's appearance in return, but unfortunately Kathleen looked great. Super-great, actually. She wasn't that much cuter than Cecily, who in moments of hard honesty would've called them both "average," but the Pruitts had a little more money to spend on clothes, makeup, and highlights for Kathleen's hair. It made a difference, one that Kathleen didn't let Cecily forget.

Outside, thunder boomed, suggesting Cecily was going to be stuck inside with Kathleen for a very long time.

"Kathleen's been asking and asking about you!" said Mrs. Pruitt, who was hugging Mom. "Just couldn't wait to catch up with her best summer bud!"

Bud. Ugh. Cecily forced a smile. "Seems like we were here only yesterday."

"Oh, Cecily," Kathleen singsonged as she gestured toward the bathroom. "Did you meet Scott?"

From the bathroom stepped Gorgeous Polite Guy, a.k.a. Scott. He had a towel slung around his shoulders, which he had apparently just used to dry his hair, which was now delectably tousled. Before Cecily could think about all the ways she would have liked to muss his hair for him, she saw, to her horror, that he was walking straight toward Kathleen—who snuggled against him in satisfaction.

In the background she could hear Kathleen's mother

saying, "Well, we thought Scott could room with Theo, if that's all right with you. He's such a nice young man—you'll love him. His parents gave their permission so I thought why not let Kathleen bring her boyfriend?"

Boyfriend. This amazing, incredible, perfect guy is Kathleen Pruitt's boyfriend. There is no justice. There is no God. Okay, maybe there's a God, but justice? None.

Kathleen smiled even more broadly. "Did *you* bring anyone along this year, Cecily?"

Cecily would've shaken her head, but Theo piped up, "I tried to bring Pudge, but they wouldn't let me. Pudge is my hamster."

Kathleen whispered to Scott, just loud enough for Cecily to overhear, "He named it after his sister."

Scott didn't laugh at Kathleen's mean little joke. He frowned, playing dumb, as though he didn't get it, though of course he must have. No, he was too polite to laugh at something so mean. Too nice. Too good. That made the situation even worse.

Kathleen had somehow managed to get her hooks into a guy who was tall, handsome, polite, *and* totally non-evil. (In other words, a guy with whom she had nothing in common.) Obviously she intended to use her new relationship to make Cecily feel as small and alone as possible. And the rain was only falling harder.

It's official, Cecily thought. *I am in hell.*

Part Two

SELF-IMPROVEMENT GOALS: REVISED

During this hellish week at the Outer Banks I will:
- continue to be nice to Theo, and never ever once give in to the temptation to ask him about Scott, because I do not care about Scott
- talk to Scott as little as possible, because I should avoid any guy who would decide to date Kathleen of his own free will
- really concentrate during the coven meetings and turn this into a learning experience, because, let's face it, as a vacation, it's already pretty much ruined
- remember that I am too good to notice the bitchery of Kathleen Pruitt, even though said

bitchery is big enough to be seen from outer
space

The women sat in a circle in the basement, a candle
flickering in the center. Acrid fumes laced the air. Cecily
was used to the smells by now, but sometimes she wondered if they couldn't use a scented candle to make their
work atmosphere a bit more pleasant. Or would any new
element disturb the energy? She'd have to ask.

Mom used a thin white switch to etch the rune patterns in the mixed ashes. She had a beautiful hand for
it—precise and delicate—and Cecily envied her mother's sure touch.

Someday I'll be that good, she promised herself.

Each woman sat with her daughter or daughters—
save for Mrs. Pruitt, because Kathleen had skipped
coven. That was unlike Kathleen, who normally liked to
use those occasions as opportunities for embarrassing
Cecily. Then again, Kathleen liked to use every occasion
to embarrass somebody or other. Cecily was grateful for
the brief break.

When the rune pattern was complete, Mom put
something in front of the small pile of ashes—a
single brown shoe, one that belonged to Cecily's
father. Everyone else put something in as well: a husband's T-shirt, a father's sunglasses. Cecily set Theo's
Game Boy atop the rest. Another couple flicks of the
switch drew lines of ash around the pile of items,

containing them within the spell.

"Time to anoint," her mother said to the circle as a whole. The other moms all nodded, and their daughters—who ranged in age from Cecily's down to a four-year-old in pigtails—scooted closer to get a better look. Then her mother added, "Try it, Cecily."

Cecily had been performing this step in the spell for a couple of months now, and sometimes for harder spells than this. But she'd never done it in front of anyone but her mother before—not even for the coven at home. She saw the mothers trade glances among themselves, surprised and not necessarily approving. Most witches were a couple years older than Cecily before they were capable of handling that kind of power.

No pressure, she thought.

She picked up the vial they'd cooked up in the autoclave late last night. The deep purple liquid within was viscous—maybe more than was ideal—but at least it would be easier to pour. Cecily pulled out the stopper and refused to wrinkle her nose at the smell. She tipped the vial forward and deftly poured a thin stream into the shape of the rune, following her mother's outline precisely. The grooves in the ash caught the fluid, and the rune of liquid began, ever so slightly, to glow.

"Very good," her mother said. Cecily felt the tension in the room ease. Her mother took the candle—a part Cecily wasn't very good at yet because she always lost her concentration when the heated wax singed her fingers. Mom didn't flinch once as she dipped the flame toward the fluid—which caught fire.

For a moment the flames leaped high—still brilliant purple, still in the shape of the rune. Then the ash caught fire too, and a smoky cloud appeared above them. There, flickering in three dimensions, were the people they'd sought with the spyglass spell: all the fathers and brothers, out watching a baseball game at a nearby sports bar. Cecily caught a glimpse of Theo stealing an onion ring from Dad's plate, and she nearly giggled.

The next thing she saw, however, wiped the smile from her face.

There was Scott—somehow even more insanely gorgeous than he'd been the day before. His arm rested around Kathleen's shoulders, and he stared at her adoringly as she filed her fingernails. Neither of them was paying any attention to the game.

Scott doesn't even like sports, Cecily thought. The guy she'd gone with briefly in the spring had wanted to spend most weekend afternoons watching televised golf, which was pretty much in a nutshell why she wasn't going out with him anymore. Not liking sports was virtually the only way in which Scott could've become more perfect, so naturally he'd gone and done it.

Finding a boyfriend who was perfect to the point of not liking sports was virtually the only way that

Kathleen Pruitt could've become even more unbearable. As much as Cecily had always loathed Kathleen, she'd never envied her before.

No doubt Kathleen knew that Cecily was jealous, and was enjoying every second of it.

Maybe she doesn't even like Scott that much, Cecily thought hopefully. *Maybe she's only with him to spite me.*

But there wasn't much chance of that. Although probably Kathleen would do anything to spite Cecily, any girl would like Scott.

Just when the sight of them together seemed to sear Cecily's eyes, the image flickered out. The flames smothered, and where the ashes had been were only a few sprinkles of dust on the basement floor. A clean working area was the sign of a spell well cast.

"Very nice," said one of the mothers, and Cecily knew the praise was for her.

The coven meeting more or less broke up at that point. This was more of an instructional session than anything else; the spyglass spell had been for demonstration purposes only, since all the women knew about the sports-bar excursion. Some of the mothers went over the finer points of the spell with the daughters as everybody got up and gathered together the items they'd taken to focus their magic, to put the things back where they belonged.

"You did fine work today," her mother said, pulling

gently at Cecily's ponytail.

"I try to pay attention." Cecily attempted to look innocent. "Instead of skipping coven. Like some people."

"Can it." Mom glanced to make sure Mrs. Pruitt hadn't heard; they were good friends, which was one reason Cecily wasn't allowed to show openly how much she loathed Kathleen.

As Cecily tucked Theo's Game Boy back into his luggage, she wondered, *Would she skip coven if it meant she could spend time with Scott? Without Kathleen?* Cecily decided she wouldn't do it often—but she'd certainly do it once.

But no. Scott wasn't perfect. Nobody was perfect. Sure he was gorgeous—and sweet and built—but he had chosen to date Kathleen. So there was one huge flaw right there. No doubt his other faults would make themselves known in time.

The guys, plus Kathleen, all returned about an hour later, after the baseball game had ended. If anything, it was raining even harder than before, which meant that Ocean's Heaven once again seemed crowded and loud. Cecily sneaked up to her room to text her friends back home for a while, but Theo wouldn't leave her alone.

"You said you would play foosball with me!"

"I did play foosball with you," Cecily said, pressing

the keypad with her thumb so her friends would read THEO BEING BRAT. "We played three games yesterday. Remember?"

"But I want to play today."

"Theo—"

"You don't like playing anymore because you can't always win now that I'm bigger." Theo folded his arms across his chest. Apparently this was her only reward for pretending to lose: an even sulkier baby brother.

"Okay, okay. Let's play." Cecily's first thought, as they headed downstairs, was to show Theo that she could in fact still beat him at foosball, absolutely *cream* him, so he wouldn't bug her about playing any longer. Then she reminded herself that being nice to Theo was just about the only vacation self-improvement goal she'd been able to keep.

In the game room a group of people were watching a DVD on the wide-screen TV, some action movie that seemed to be mostly about things blowing up. Her father sat in the center munching on pretzels. With a cheery smile Ms. Giordano called to them, "You kids having fun?"

"I can beat Cecily at foosball now!" Theo proclaimed. Cecily gritted her teeth.

Then she heard, "Well, then, maybe I should help Cecily out." She turned to see Scott put his hands on the side of the foosball table. "What do you say, Theo? Can I play on Cecily's side? Give her a chance?"

"Well—" Theo clearly didn't like the idea of relinquishing the upper hand.

"I'm not very good at foosball," Scott confessed. "So it's not like I'd be that much help."

Theo smiled. "Okay, then."

Cecily went to the foosball table, so she and Scott stood side to side. This was the closest they'd been since he'd helped carry their luggage. She glanced around for Kathleen, who was nowhere to be seen, and Cecily wasn't about to ask where she was. "You don't know what you've gotten yourself in for," she said. "Theo's pretty fierce."

Theo spun some of the foosball men around, obviously hoping to prove her point.

"I'm strong." Scott kept his face completely straight. "I can take it." The glint in his eyes told Cecily that he'd lose the game on purpose, just like she would have on her own—which would make Theo's ego almost unbearable, but would also make him really happy.

Gorgeous, sweet, built, and nice to little kids. Okay, I have to figure out what's wrong with this guy before it drives me insane.

"How did you meet Kathleen?" Cecily said as Theo dropped the ball into the table.

"At school," Scott said, giving the ball a whack. "I'd

seen her around all year, but we never got to know each other. Then after spring break, the first time I laid eyes on her—it was like I was seeing her for the first time. You know?"

"Mmm." Cecily concentrated on the game for a second, because that seemed like the best way not to actually gag out loud.

Scott continued, "It's sort of funny, though. We have this great relationship, even though we don't enjoy the same things. I used to think that was impossible."

"What kind of stuff do you like to do?" Cecily felt she could guess Kathleen's interests: reading gossip magazines, bleaching her roots, tormenting the innocent.

"You would never guess my number-one hobby."

"I'm not even going to try. Just tell me."

"I like to cook." Surprised, Cecily glanced at Scott instead of the foosball table, which gave Theo a chance to score. As Theo cheered himself, Scott laughed. "You don't think guys should cook? You don't look old-fashioned."

"I'm not," she said. "It's just—you know—I *love* to cook."

Scott nodded. "You get it, then. I was thinking about maybe trying to become a chef someday."

At home on Cecily's desk, where most of her friends would've kept college catalogs of prospective universities, she had brochures from every top cooking school in the nation and a couple in Paris. "Oh," she said weakly. "Me too. That's—"

"A huge coincidence, huh?" Scott gave her a conspiratorial grin. "I'm crazy about Kathleen, but I don't think she can even make toast."

Cecily's absolute, ultimate dream for her future was one she'd never seriously expected to come to pass, because dreams were dreams and reality was reality and she felt people were better off understanding the difference. But it was still fun to dream, so she'd imagined falling in love with a gorgeous, sweet, built guy who loved cooking absolutely as much as she did. Then they would open their own restaurant together, and it would be a huge success, and Cecily and the future Mr. Cecily would be incredibly happy cooking side by side.

And Scott was the very first guy she'd ever met who'd made her realize that dream might not actually be impossible.

"It's great that you know what you want," Scott said. "Too many people don't."

"Exactly! They keep saying that at our age, you don't have to make up your mind. But shouldn't you *want* to make up your mind?"

"So you have some direction. It's all so much clearer that way."

"Absolutely."

"Hey," Theo said loudly. "You're not even paying attention!"

Cecily blushed. Scott laughed and rumpled Theo's hair. "Sorry, buddy. We were just trying to get you off your guard, so maybe we'd stand a chance." Then he glanced back at Cecily, and something about the affection in his blue eyes made her bones seem to liquefy. She leaned against the table, telling herself that kissing another girl's boyfriend in the middle of a crowded room wasn't a good idea. Even though her body seemed to be swaying toward him, beyond her control—

"What's going on in here?" Kathleen wandered in, holding her hands out in front of her, fingers splayed. Her nails gleamed wetly of red polish.

Theo said, "Scott's helping Cecily, but I can still beat them both!"

Kathleen sighed. "I guess there's no helping Cecily, is there?"

"You were doing your nails?" Cecily said. "Again?"

"Yes." Apparently Kathleen didn't even register that as an insult. "This color is much better, I think. I want to do my toes too. Scott, lend me a hand, okay?"

"Okay." Scott winked at Theo. "You and I are going to have a rematch later. Cecily—good talking to you."

"You too."

Already Scott had turned away—willing to drop

everything to give Kathleen a pedicure. He had to be absolutely crazy about her to do something like that.

How can he be so into her? Cecily thought in despair. *How can any guy so right for me be in love with the peroxide piranha? This just can't be for real.*

Wait—THIS CAN'T BE FOR REAL.

Cecily's eyes went wide. Adrenaline made her heart thump crazily, and nothing around her seemed entirely genuine. Although she remained at the foosball table occasionally spinning her men, she couldn't pay any attention to what was going on; for once Theo beat her fair and square.

As soon as the game ended, Cecily hurried upstairs to her room. She needed a couple of seconds of privacy to think. Because if what she suspected was true—

It isn't. It couldn't be. Kathleen Pruitt's awful, but not even she could be that awful. Could she?

Being a bitch was one thing. Actually misusing the Craft to force someone to fall in love with her—that was something else altogether. That was serious. That was *bad*. Maybe it wasn't as awful as murder, but Cecily had been brought up to believe that subverting someone's will was more or less in the same general category.

That would explain why Kathleen had skipped the afternoon coven meeting too—the enchantment on Scott would've been a powerful one, so much so that traces of it might have lingered and affected the coven's work. Kathleen's cover would have been blown, and all the other witches would've known what a horrible thing she'd done.

The thought of Kathleen publicly shamed gave Cecily a little thrill of satisfaction, and almost instantly she felt ashamed.

If you really thought she'd done it, you wouldn't be happy, Cecily told herself. *You'd be horrified, and worried about Scott. But you don't really think Kathleen's that wicked. You just enjoy thinking that she could be, because it's easier than thinking that Scott might actually be in love with her for real. Which he obviously is. So get over it.*

But the idea wouldn't quite go away.

Finally, Cecily decided that she'd prove to herself how ridiculous her theory was. Quickly she pulled her Craft supplies from beneath the bed and grabbed a small plastic spray bottle from her luggage. On hot days at the beach she filled the bottle with water so she could cool down while remaining in the sun; obviously, she wouldn't be needing it for that anytime soon.

A simple solution would be best. Something she didn't have to cook up. Thinking fast, Cecily realized that a couple of the elixirs from this morning might do the trick if she poured them together in the right proportions. It was difficult without a measuring cup, but she managed to get it close.

First she tested the solution, tiptoeing into Theo's

room. Cecily determinedly didn't look at Scott's things on the bottom bunk; instead, she took the Game Boy she'd used for the spyglass spell. After glancing down the hall to make sure that nobody was watching, she squirted the bottle over the Game Boy.

The mist of liquid turned briefly brilliant pink—proving the Game Boy had been the subject of a spell or enchantment in the recent past.

Cecily nodded, satisfied. If nothing else, at least she'd learned how to work up a spell-detection elixir on short notice.

Are you actually going to spray this on Scott? she asked herself. *What are you going to do when nothing happens? Remember, he'll also think you're a complete weirdo who goes around stalking guys with squirt bottles of pink crap.*

"Hey, everybody!" Mr. Silverberg called. "Who wants to go out for pizza?"

"Thank god!" shouted another of the dads, and everyone laughed. Cecily wasn't the only one who had cabin fever, apparently.

And if they were all headed outside that gave Cecily her chance. Nobody would notice a few drops of water in the middle of a driving rainstorm.

She tucked the spray bottle in the pocket of her jean jacket as everybody got ready to go. Theo, always restless, ran out into the rain before anybody else, and Mom had to chase after him with an umbrella. Kathleen hurried out next, her own umbrella in hand, whining about what the humidity was doing to her hair. Scott was about to follow her, but Cecily grabbed his arm at the door. "Oh, Scott—" she said casually. "Did you happen to see Theo's Game Boy? We should really take it along tonight so he won't get bored."

"Yeah, I think I saw that in our room." Scott smiled at her. "You're a good sister, you know?"

As Scott jogged inside to search their room, Cecily took her own sweet time slipping into her sandals. After she had fastened the last buckle, the only people left in the house were she and Scott.

"Come on, you two!" Dad shouted through the cracked-open window of their rental car.

Scott emerged, Game Boy in hand. They both dashed out into the rain, and Cecily made sure to be a few steps behind him so that nobody would be able to see what she was about to do. Quickly she took the spray bottle, reminded herself that this was slightly nuts, and squeezed the trigger.

The mist turned pink, sparkling for one moment before it vanished.

Cecily froze. For a moment she simply stood there, rain pouring down on her; in her shock, she couldn't feel anything.

Kathleen had done it. She actually had done it. She had broken one of the Craft's strongest laws.

Scott doesn't really love her.

"Cecily!" Dad yelled. "What are you doing?"

Haltingly Cecily managed to make her way to the car and get inside. By the time she shut the door behind her, she was sopping wet. "Ugh. Honestly," Kathleen huffed. She sat in the center of the backseat curled next to Scott, who was smiling at her sort of vacantly. "Stop dripping on me, Cecily."

Cecily said nothing. She couldn't even look at Kathleen for fear of revealing that she knew the truth.

It was funny, sort of: she'd always thought Kathleen Pruitt was a horrible person. And now it turned out she hadn't known the half of it. Kathleen wasn't just vain, shallow, and cruel—she was really and truly evil.

Cecily stole a sideways glance. Kathleen sat with her head against Scott's shoulder, and she smiled smugly when she saw Cecily watching.

Somehow Cecily managed to smile back, but she was thinking, *Smile while you can. Because you won't get away with it.*

Part Three

SELF-IMPROVEMENT GOALS:
NOW TOTALLY REVISED DUE TO
STATE OF EMERGENCY

At this time of crisis I will:
- talk to Mom about how best to handle freeing Scott from the enchantment, because breaking a magical tie strong enough to make a great guy like him fall for Kathleen is probably out of my league
- resist the urge to say "I told you so" to Mom when the evil of Kathleen Pruitt is finally demonstrated to be objective, verifiable fact
- enjoy my moment of triumph over The Loathsome One, but not so much that I don't pay attention to the enchantment-breaking,

because that is going to be high-level magic of
the first degree

"Cecily, honestly." Mom folded her arms. "We're out having a good time, and you're making another of your lists on a napkin?"

"We need to talk," Cecily said, quickly tucking the napkin in her skirt pocket.

"No, we need to enjoy ourselves." Mom put her hands on Cecily's shoulders, pushing her to turn and look at the small stage in the corner of Mario's Karaoke Pizzeria. Several of the fathers from the group, with Theo standing in front of Dad, were all bellowing, "We Are the Champions."

This would normally have been enough to make Cecily cringe with embarrassment, but larger concerns were at stake. "Mom, it's about Kathleen. She—I—well, we have to do something, because—"

"Do what, Cecily? Break it up every time you two start to squabble?"

"That's not what I'm talking about."

Her mother didn't seem to hear her. "You act like Kathleen's the most horrible human being who ever walked the face of the earth. You've always acted like that, ever since the two of you were four years old and she knocked over your sand castle."

Cecily had been proud of that sand castle. "But Mom—"

"I don't want to hear it. Yes, I know she says catty things; I have ears too, you know. Kathleen has never been as mature as you are, and I guess it's going to take her a few more years to catch up. But I really wish you could act like an adult and let that kind of thing roll off your back." Mom lowered her voice. "I realize that you seem very . . . well, *taken* with Scott, so it must be difficult for you. But that's no excuse to keep obsessing about Kathleen Pruitt. Now come join the rest of us, all right? You don't have to sing if you'll just listen to everybody else."

Mom walked off, leaving Cecily alone at the end of the long table, her cheeks flaming with both anger and shame.

The anger was because her mother hadn't listened to her. The shame was because Cecily knew it was her fault Mom hadn't listened.

Every year, as long as she could remember, she had griped about Kathleen. She'd tried to skip the Outer Banks vacation altogether; once she'd locked herself in her room when Kathleen arrived; she even remembered holding her breath as a very small child until her mother agreed that she and Kathleen didn't have to sit next to each other at dinner. Their dislike had always been mutual—but Kathleen had never made a scene.

Too late Cecily realized that she'd complained about Kathleen so often, and for so many trivial (if *entirely valid*) reasons, that not even her mother would listen to her on the subject any longer.

The witch who cried wolf, she thought. *Great. Now Kathleen's actually gone evil for real, and nobody will believe me.*

She glanced at the group and saw Scott sitting next to Kathleen, a vague smile on his face. He squirted ketchup on her French fries in the shape of a heart. Clearly, for the sake of his dignity, something had to be done.

Cecily would just have to do it herself.

"We Are the Champions" concluded, with the men holding their fists over their heads and Theo jumping up and down with excitement. Everybody in the place applauded, and Cecily absentmindedly joined in. She almost didn't hear the announcer say, "Next up is— Cecily Harper!"

Wait—what?

"Cecily Harper? Where is she?" The announcer peered out into the group, then smiled as Theo pointed out his sister. "Let's give the lovely young lady a hand!"

Running did not seem to be an option, and it was too late to hide. Cecily rose, unsure what to think—until she saw Kathleen hiding her smirk beneath one newly manicured hand.

She signed me up for this. Why wasn't I watching her more closely?

"Go for it, honey!" Dad yelled, clapping vigorously.

He and Mom looked so happy that she'd decided to join in.

Cecily cast a glance at the crowd—at least one hundred people in sandals and T-shirts, all of them slightly stir-crazy from the bad weather, waiting to hear her sing. At this point she figured they were pretty starved for entertainment. She wasn't a particularly gifted singer, but she didn't suck either. Depending on the song, maybe she could get through it. As Kathleen-Pruitt-Brand Evil went, this wasn't all that bad.

Hesitantly she made her way to the stage and took the microphone in hand. The prompter screen came up with the lyrics to the song that was about to play—the song Kathleen had chosen in her name.

In horror she saw the chorus: "My hump, my hump, my lovely lady lumps."

Gripping the microphone so tightly she could have used it for a club, Cecily forced a smile onto her face and thought, *This means war.*

They got back to the beach houses fairly late that night. The rain hadn't stopped, but it had finally tapered to a light drizzle. Nobody needed umbrellas to get from the cars to the houses. Cecily walked with Theo, who was unsteady on his feet; he wasn't used to staying up to this hour. Although Cecily was fairly tired herself, her mind was far too wired for her to fall asleep.

I need to break the enchantment on Scott. I really don't have any idea how to accomplish that. I can't count on Mom to help me out. So what do I do?

The best possible resource was her mother's Book of Shadows.

Every witch kept a Book of Shadows. Cecily wasn't old enough to have started hers yet—that began when apprenticeship ended. Nobody ever completed a Book of Shadows; witches worked on theirs throughout their entire lives. The books contained lists of spells but not only that; they would also hold each story of how the witch had learned the spell, when and how and why she had used it, and what the results were each time.

When she was younger, Cecily had planned to keep her Book of Shadows in electronic format—that would make it harder to destroy and easier to update and organize. (She sometimes thought dreamily of the Excel spreadsheets she could create of magical ingredients.) However, she'd learned that the book itself was important. It was to be kept near any time a powerful spell was being performed, and over time the nearness to magic seeped into the pages. The Book of Shadows of an old powerful witch almost had powers of its own.

Walking up and saying, "Hi, Mom, can I borrow your Book of Shadows?" was completely out of the question. Cecily had been allowed to look at it before but only in her mother's company and only on special occasions.

That meant she'd have to steal it.

Well, not "steal." Borrow. It seemed better to think of this as borrowing; after all, Mom would get her Book of Shadows back. She just wouldn't know that it had been gone.

Everyone was getting ready for bed, which meant they were wearing their pajamas in the hall and pretending not to mind that other people were using the bathrooms. Cecily put on a T-shirt and a pair of yoga pants—believable as sleepwear but also ideal for sneaking around the house, or sneaking out of it.

She wandered through the house, trying to look casual, which shouldn't have been so difficult in a T-shirt and yoga pants. *Mom and Dad, where are you? Please don't already be in bed—*

They weren't. They were sitting in the front room, each drinking a glass of wine, being sort of disgustingly mushy with each other. Cecily averted her eyes, the better to avoid witnessing the dreaded parental make-out session. The point was they were distracted, which gave her a window of opportunity.

Quickly she tiptoed down the hall toward her parents' bedroom. Nobody saw her except Theo, who was rubbing his eyes and probably too tired to notice.

Cecily peered around the bedroom, considering and

then rejecting possible hiding places. Dad might look in any of the drawers or under the bed, so her mother wouldn't have put the book there. Same thing with any of the suitcases. It would have to be someplace really safe, yet unexpected.

Cecily's eyes lit up as she noticed the shadow box above the bed. It was merely decoration—a kitschy beach scene, which was pretty much the kind of thing that had to count as style in Ocean's Heaven—but it stood out from the wall a bit, and it was big enough. . . .

She tugged the shadow box from the wall, and the Book of Shadows flopped onto the bed.

Just when it looked like she'd pulled it off, Cecily heard her mother in the hallway. "You know, it's kind of sexy when you sing."

Dad laughed softly. "I would've spent all night on stage if I'd known that."

Horror froze Cecily to the spot. What was worse: being caught stealing Mom's Book of Shadows or having to hear her parents flirt? She'd never find out, because she was about to do both at the same time, which was as bad as it could possibly get.

Then she heard Theo. "Mommy, Daddy, come read me a story!"

"You want a story before bed? You haven't asked for one in a while." Dad sounded affectionate. "We don't want to keep Scott awake."

"He's off kissing Kathleen," Theo said scornfully. "Come read to me!"

Their footsteps approached the doorway—then went past it, heading toward Theo. Cecily caught her breath for a second before she clasped the Book of Shadows to her chest and sneaked out.

As she went, she looked behind her. Mom had Theo in her arms as they walked toward his room. He smiled at Cecily from over their mother's shoulder and winked.

I can't believe it. Theo saved me! Her little brother couldn't possibly have guessed why she needed to be in their parents' room, but he'd covered for her anyway. Just because. It was definitely the least bratty moment of his life to date.

Cecily grinned at her brother, proud that at least one of her self-improvement goals had paid off.

Now to fulfill the most important goal of them all: taking Kathleen down.

Part Four

DISENCHANTMENT SPELL CHECKLIST

✓ moth's wings
  red wine—located in wet bar of beach house
✓ purified ash
  broken glass—smash a glass in kitchen, leave a
  couple dollars for house owners
✓ essence of verity
  cauldron—will improvise
✓ crushed beetle shells
  virgin's blood—depressingly, can provide this
  myself

The wind whipped in from the ocean, chilling Cecily
as she sat on the still-damp sand. Although the rain had

finally stopped, the skies overhead remained ominously clouded, without any stars.

Her mother's Book of Shadows sat next to her on a beach towel. Although it wasn't decorated as elaborately as some witches preferred—Mom liked to keep things simple—the book possessed a kind of power just sitting there. Maybe it was Cecily's imagination, but the pale gray cover seemed to glow a little even without any moonlight.

She could have done this research inside, but that would have been too comfortable: warm and cozy with a lamp to read by. The temptation to discover all of Mom's spells would've been too great. Cecily didn't feel guilty for stealing the Book of Shadows, because this was important, but she would lose the moral high ground if she abused this opportunity.

Besides, being out of the cramped house with its silly decorations was a good thing. Cecily found the cool night air and the roaring ocean clarified her thinking. For instance, she'd stopped reveling in the shame this would cause Kathleen and worrying about how Mom would react when she found out about the unauthorized use of her Book of Shadows. Instead Cecily was thinking about Scott.

What will the end of the enchantment be like for him? she wondered. The Book of Shadows didn't say. *Will he*

simply not care much about Kathleen anymore, and won-
der what he ever saw in her? Or will it be more dramatic
than that? And if it is dramatic, will he realize he's been
enchanted?

Cecily had been the subject of some harmless enchantments a few times; that was a standard part of a witch's education, finding out how it felt. When the enchantment broke, the feeling was unmistakable: as sudden and powerful as the drop in a roller coaster after it had climbed a hill. You came smashing down to earth, and you *knew* that something unnatural had just happened to you.

Even somebody who had never heard of the Craft might well understand that they'd been the subject of magic. That was one reason enchantments were to be used sparingly, if at all.

If Scott realized the truth, then what?

Probably there was an answer lurking deep within the pages of Mom's Book of Shadows, but Cecily wasn't going to look for it. In her heart she had always believed that men could hear and accept the truth about witchcraft. (Maybe not *all* men—but all women couldn't hear it either, could they?) Somehow her mother could live with lying to her father forever and ever, but Cecily had never wanted that for herself.

The guy of her dreams—the chef who wanted to

open a restaurant with her—he would know not only that Cecily practiced the Craft, but would also see how amazing it was. He would be proud of her power. He would support her no matter what.

Could Scott actually be that guy?

Her heart thumped crazily in her chest. One way or another Cecily was going to find out.

The next morning wasn't sunny exactly, but at least it wasn't raining. Despite the chill in the air and the thick cloud cover, pretty much everyone headed to the beach. Theo ran down the hallway in his swim trunks and neon green flippers, yelling, "Cecily! You have to go swimming with us!"

"I'll catch up," Cecily promised as she shimmied into her black bikini. "It won't be long."

She stared at herself in the mirror. Had she once been afraid of something as little as wearing a swimsuit? Compared to what was at stake today that seemed so small.

Besides—she looked good.

Cecily sauntered out of her room, acting casual, with a large beach towel folded over one arm in such a way that it disguised what she was holding in her hand: the spray bottle, which was filled with an all but complete elixir for the disenchantment spell.

Already the house was almost empty—except for Scott, who was rubbing sunblock on his shoulders. It took all Cecily's self-control not to ask him if he needed help. "Hey," he said. "Kathleen and I are about to hit the beach. Want to join us?"

"She doesn't want to!" Kathleen yelled from her room.

Cecily smiled. "I think it's a little cold for a dip in the ocean, don't you?"

"Yeah, but there's no way I'm spending a week on the Outer Banks without going swimming once," Scott said. He glanced at her bikini—just a glance—but it was encouraging.

Casually, as if the idea had only just occurred to her, Cecily said, "Hey, what about the hot tub on the deck? Warm water, Jacuzzi jets—way better than freezing our butts off in the surf."

Scott had a slow, warm smile that made her feel sort of gooey inside. "You know, that sounds great."

"You and Kathleen get comfortable. I have to check on Theo, but I'll stop by the hot tub on my way out."

Cauldron—check.

She walked toward the wet bar but glanced over her shoulder to see Scott headed toward the deck. Never before had she realized even a guy's *back* could be sexy.

Not that Kathleen wasn't one hundred percent evil to do this to you, she thought, *but I do at least get her motivation.*

Once they were outside Cecily got to work. Corkscrews looked simple enough to use, but she'd never attempted to handle one before, so opening the red wine took much longer than she'd planned. The delay made the process even more suspenseful. If her mother walked in and saw Cecily uncorking a bottle of booze, she wouldn't get a chance to explain why she really needed it. She wouldn't survive that long.

Finally the cork slid loose with a pop. The red wine smelled sort of stinky to Cecily—maybe this stuff had gone to vinegar. Probably it wouldn't matter for the spell, though.

She poured a thin stream of wine into the spray bottle. A wisp of periwinkle blue smoke drifted upward, glittering and eerie.

The smoke needed to be darker than that—the magic, more powerful.

With a shaky hand Cecily took a glass tumbler from the bar and held it over the sink. She was scared now, and she told herself that it was stupid to be scared of pain. Did she want to be like Theo, whining and crying before he got a shot at the pediatrician's?

But it wasn't the prospect of pain that frightened her. It was the reality of performing this spell—by far the most powerful Cecily had ever attempted on her own. She had no idea what would happen if she got it wrong, but she strongly suspected it wouldn't be good.

Enough, she told herself sternly. Turning her face to protect her eyes, Cecily threw the glass into the sink. It shattered with a crash, and she felt a sharp jab against her palm. Well, at least she wouldn't have to actually slice her skin open.

Cecily added a few small shards of glass to the mix, then held the open spray bottle beneath her trembling hand and a few drops of her blood fell inside. With each drop the smoke puffed again, darkening into deeper blue, then into purple, and finally almost into black. That looked more like it.

Showtime.

She strode onto the deck, hoping she looked confident. Kathleen and Scott sat alone in the hot tub, and Kathleen had hooked her legs over his, as though she were about to sit in his lap. When Cecily stepped out, Kathleen looked over with a scowl. "Uh, don't you need to play with your baby brother or something?"

"Soon," Cecily said. "Not now."

Scott grinned and gestured toward the spray bottle. "What's that?"

A gust of cool wind tossed Cecily's hair and made her shiver. "Your freedom."

Kathleen's eyes opened wide. She knew. It was now or never.

Whispering the incantation, Cecily yanked off the top of the spray bottle and dumped the contents into the hot tub.

The currents caught it, creating a spiral of blue-black that widened every second. Instead of diluting within the water the elixir darkened the contents of the hot tub until it looked as if Scott and Kathleen were sitting in ink. Thick smoke began bubbling at the surface and tumbling over the sides. The air turned sulfuric, and Cecily felt as if she could hardly breathe.

"What the—" Scott tried to push himself out of the Jacuzzi, but he didn't make it, because that was when everything exploded.

Not for real, with bits of tub and deck and Kathleen spraying everywhere. But it felt like an explosion anyway. A shock wave smashed outward, shaking them all and thundering like a sonic boom. Little arcs of static electricity vaulted through the air. Kathleen started screaming, and Cecily didn't blame her.

Then it was over. Scott slumped down in the tub as if unconscious, but Cecily jumped forward to catch his head. "Scott?" Her voice shook. "Scott, are you okay?"

"Yeah." He sat upright, blinking slowly. His expression looked dazed. "What was that?"

"You don't need to know!" Kathleen clambered out

of the hot tub. Her whole body shook, and some of her hair literally stood on end from the energy in the air. "Scott, come on."

Cecily said, "He's not going anywhere with you."

"Who are you to say? Scott, come with me!" Kathleen held a hand out to him, but he didn't budge.

His expression still looked dazed. No, Cecily thought the correct word was "vacant." Like there was nobody home. Had she hurt him?

Then the Jacuzzi jets came on, and Scott grinned a lazy, stupid sort of smile that Cecily had never seen before. "Dude, hot tubs crack me up. You know why?"

Cecily cocked her head. "Uh, no?"

He said, "Because when the jets make the bubbles, it's like somebody farted."

"Are you sure you feel okay?" Cecily said. "Because you—you don't sound like yourself."

Scott laughed the kind of laugh that sounded like a donkey's bray. "Guess what? I'm farting right now! And you can't tell!"

Cecily stumbled away from the hot tub, backing toward the other side of the deck. Something was wrong with him; he wasn't at all the kind of person he'd been before. Had she done something wrong when she broke the enchantment? Had she hurt Scott?

Kathleen wiped angry tears from her cheeks. "You *ruined* him!"

The truth hit Cecily. "You didn't just make him like you. The enchantment altered his personality too, so he'd be the perfect guy for you." *Or for me*, she thought, remembering how Scott had seemed so ideal when he was with her—and how his personality had seemed to change the moment Kathleen walked into the room. Why hadn't she seen it before? The real Scott was this guy: slack-jawed, stupid, and completely unconcerned with anything around him. He wasn't even paying any attention to their conversation.

"If you had the guts to borrow your mom's Book of Shadows, you'd know how to do real magic too," Kathleen jeered. She advanced upon Cecily, who pressed her back against the deck railing. What other evil spells could Kathleen have learned? What else might she be willing to do? Cecily wanted to think she could defend herself, but more than that she wanted to run for help. Yet Kathleen stood between her and any escape. "Scott was perfect, and he can be perfect again, because you're about to get out of my way."

"No, she isn't," Mrs. Pruitt said sternly. She stood in the doorway of the deck, with all the mothers standing just behind her. Their faces were grave. "Kathleen, come talk with me."

Kathleen's face changed then, from its default setting (evil) to something Cecily had never seen before:

real fear. Obviously the mothers had recognized the breaking of an enchantment; just as obviously they'd overheard enough to realize what Kathleen had done. Nobody was wielding any magic; they didn't have to. The moms' power eclipsed anything Cecily or Kathleen could do.

And at long last the evil reign of Kathleen Pruitt had come to a crashing end.

"What will happen to her?" Cecily asked later as she and her mother walked on the beach.

"Kathleen will never be allowed to practice magic again. She'll never be given the right incantations to start a Book of Shadows, and her supplies and instruments will have to be destroyed. We can't erase what she already knows, but from now on she's cut out of this or any coven. It's going to be hard on her mother, but rules are rules." They went on silently for a few steps before Mom said, "I'm proud of you for not gloating."

Cecily was pretty sure she'd get in some quality gloating later, but the shock of it all was too new for that. "All that smoke, the boom—Dad has to have seen it."

"We told the guys the Jacuzzi shorted out. No more hot-tubbing on this trip, I'm afraid."

It would be a long time before Cecily could look at

a Jacuzzi the same way again, so no loss there. "And Scott?"

"Doesn't know what hit him. Or care, I think."

They looked together toward Ocean's Heaven. Scott sat with Theo on the front steps that led to the sand. He chugged half a can of root beer then belched Theo's name, which made Theo laugh and applaud. Cecily sighed.

Mom said, "You tried to warn me about Kathleen last night. I should have heard you out. In future I will."

"Thanks, Mom."

"Which means you will never again have any excuse for laying hands on my Book of Shadows without my permission."

"Understood."

Mom tugged fondly at the end of Cecily's ponytail. "You took a big risk, you know—and not just attempting the spell on your own. If Scott were any more—let's say *inquisitive*, he would have realized that he had been under an enchantment. He would have realized that magic is real. Covering our tracks at that point would've been hard work. That you couldn't have done alone."

"Why do we have to lie to them? Don't you ever wish Dad knew the truth? Don't you think he'd love you even more when he realized what an amazing witch you are?"

For a moment Mom was silent. The only sound was the roar of the ocean. At last she said, "Today of all days I'd think you would understand the importance of obeying the rules."

That wasn't an answer, but Cecily knew it was as close as she would get. She hugged Mom before jogging down to the shoreline. The waves were cold and foamy against her toes.

Someday, Cecily thought. *Someday I'll find a guy who can live with the truth. Just because that's not Scott doesn't mean a guy like that isn't out there.*

At least her summer vacation wasn't entirely ruined. Cecily had a few days left to enjoy herself, which she felt she richly deserved.

SELF-IMPROVEMENT GOALS: REVISED

During my remaining vacation time I will:

- resist gloating over Kathleen's downfall, at least while there are witnesses around
- swim for at least two hours a day
- see if the moms now respect me enough to teach me some serious Craft mojo
- beat Theo at foosball just once for the sake of my personal dignity

- walk three miles on the beach each morning
- see about tennis lessons
- see about horseback riding lessons
- basically, stay outdoors as much as humanly possible

Then thunder rolled in the distance, and raindrops began to spatter onto the sand.

Cecily groaned as she ran for shelter. *Well, maybe next year.*

The Law of Suspects

MAUREEN JOHNSON

"I hate vacation," I said.

My sister, Marylou, was in the rocking chair by the window, twisting her short, rust-colored hair around her finger absently, her *DSM-IV* open in front of her. The *DSM-IV*, in case you've never heard of it, is *The Diagnostic and Statistical Manual of Mental Health Disorders (Fourth Edition)*. Marylou had just finished her first year as a psychology major, which meant that her favorite time waster was diagnosing me with every ailment in the book—literally. So it was a mistake saying this kind of thing to her.

"Lack of interest in things normal people find enjoyable," she said. "That's depression, Charlie."

"'Normal people'?" I repeated.

"Well, that's not the term we like to use, actually...."

she said, even though she had just used it.

"Who is this *we*?"

"Mental health professionals."

The last thing Marylou was was a mental health professional. She was a barista with two semesters of intro psych under her belt.

"I see," I said. "A mental health professional. You *also* serve lattes. So are you *also* the president of Starbucks? Is that what that means?"

"Shut up, Charlie."

Page flip, page flip, page flip.

"And why are you so busy trying to diagnose *me*?" I asked, swatting away a fly that kept trying to land on my nose. "You were reading that on the plane when that guy next to me tried to stab me with his fork. You didn't give *him* a label."

"That's because he didn't try to stab you," she said placidly. "You were lying."

See, this is something that haunts me. I used to lie a lot. Or, I exaggerated a lot. I guess I was bored, and my little embellishments made the world so much more interesting. I have to say, I was really good at it. I could fool anyone. They were harmless lies too. I didn't hurt anyone with them. The little dog that chased me down the street could be bigger, perhaps rabid. I didn't just drop my ice cream while it was windy—I was hit by a freak tornado.

But lying is bad. I know this. And even though my lies weren't evil, they still caused all kinds of problems and made some people not trust me, so I gave it up, cold turkey, at the start of freshman year. I've been on the wagon for about three years now.

But do I get any credit for this? No. I guess it's like having a criminal past: no one ever really trusts you again. Like, if you were a robber, and you stopped robbing and totally re-created yourself and everyone knew it . . . still, no one will let you carry the big cash deposit to the bank.

And the guy in seat 56E really *did* try to stab me with his fork. I think this was because he thought I stole his Air France headphones while he was napping, which I didn't. The stewardess didn't give him any because he was sleeping. Marylou and I just used our own headphones on the flight, and she ended up sticking her Air France pair in my seatback pocket when she got up to go to the bathroom, so when Mr. 56E snorted himself awake halfway over the Atlantic, he stared at the two pairs of headphones I had in front of me. His mouth said nothing, but his eyes said, "Thief." When his tray came, he got out his fork with a lot more force than necessary and narrowly missed my arm. He was weird the entire flight. He got up about a dozen times to do yoga in the back of the plane by the exit door. And he was reading a book on *yogurt making* for most of the time.

But did Marylou spend any time on this paragon of sanity?

No.

Just me.

To be fair, we had nothing else to do at this particular moment when we had cycled through the disorders and gotten around to depression. Maybe I was depressed. I had every reason to be.

Marylou and I had been in France for three days, and it really wasn't going according to plan. Our mother is technically French, but her parents moved to America when she was only four. As a result, we had lots of French relatives who had been badgering my mom for years and years to send little Marie-Louise and Charlotte to see the land of their ancestors. Our cousin Claude, in particular, wanted us to come. Claude was some kind of big man in advertising in Paris and had done this ad that had babies in little suits of armor that apparently everyone *loved*. He had an apartment in the middle of town, and he wanted nothing more than to show his young cousins around.

Marylou and I were all in favor of the idea, because who doesn't want to go and stay in Paris for four weeks? That was the plan: the entire month of August. Marylou had just finished her first year of college, and I was about to be a senior in high school, so it seemed like we were old enough and young enough, and the Time Was

Right, and there was a special on Air France tickets.

So finally we were sent, and we landed in Paris, and there was Claude, who was about six foot eleven and blond and friendly. We spent one night in his apartment in Paris, sleeping off our jet lag in the guest room. We woke up expecting to take on the city and see the Eiffel Tower and ride down the street on scooters eating cheese. We wanted to embrace the life our fabulous French cousin wanted so much to show us.

Except that Claude said *non non non*, no one in Paris stays there over August. It was too hot and horrible and didn't we want to go to the country? We didn't, but we said we did to be polite. It really didn't matter what we answered, because Claude had already rented a house in Provence to show us real French life. We were leaving that afternoon. And then Claude got a call. Something had gone wrong with the babies in the little suits of armor, and he would have to fix something, and we could just go, and he would catch a later train as soon as he could, and the landlord would be there to meet us and hooray for France!

So, less than twenty-four hours after our arrival, Marylou and I were put on a train to the French countryside, with no Claude. It was a nice enough ride, which we spent staring out the window and ordering small glasses of wine for seven Euros each because we were allowed to, and we still had jet lag, and we almost missed our stop.

We were that confused and dopey. But Marylou, being Marylou, made a heroic leap for our bags, and we actually made it off the train instead of riding on until we hit Italy or the ocean or the end of the world.

Outside the station, a man in a small blue car was waiting for us. He was white-haired, looked furious, and spoke no English—but seemed to know who we were. That, and the complete lack of other possible landlords around, was enough for us to go with him. Our enormous suitcases didn't really fit in his car, so we had to get in first, and then they were piled in on top of us, pinning us to the molten-hot seats.

Along the ride he thrust a government ID at us and we learned his name was Erique. Erique had a terrible cough that would shake him so hard he would lose control of the car for a second and we would weave hilariously around the road. Marylou and I both knew about three dozen French words between us, not enough for any kind of meaningful sentence, but every once in a while we would try to charm and entertain Erique by saying things like "hot" and "train" and "Paris" and "tree" in no particular order or context. He looked at us sadly through the rearview mirror whenever we spoke, so we stopped.

We passed through the village itself, which was as quaint and beautiful as anything you could possibly want from the French countryside. People were coming out of the bakery with long loaves of bread, drinking at tables outside of a café with a red awning. There were tiny French children circling on bikes, old men sitting by an ancient central fountain, hills in the far distance. The only things that disrupted the tranquil, language-textbook perfection of it all were an ambulance and police car with silently blinking lights parked in front of one of the picturesque houses. A small cluster of paramedics and officers placidly smoked and talked by an open front door, some leaning on an empty gurney. In this town even the emergencies were handled with languid grace.

We drove right through the village, off the nice paved roads onto much bumpier ones that passed through olive groves. Then we went off the pavement entirely and onto a pitted dirt road to nowhere and nothing. We were hot and crushed and shaken around for another fifteen minutes, when Erique turned down an even narrower nonroad and a house materialized from between the branches.

The house was made of a creamy white stone, with massive duck-egg blue shutters on all the windows. It stood alone against a backdrop of trees, trees, and more trees, along with the occasional rosemary or lavender bush. Walking down the gravel path that led to it, you were pretty much knocked over by the sweet smell of the herbs baking in the sun, and then you went under the thick canopy of green that shielded the house. Off to the side there was a stream that actually gurgled and had about ten million tiny black frogs hopping around.

Erique walked us all around our new French home, opening doors, turning on fans, picking up the occasional spider or frog and flicking it out the window. The house looked like it had been redecorated once every decade, starting in maybe 1750 and ending around 1970. The furniture was all big and heavy, like something out of *The Hobbit*. Some of the rooms were wood paneled, but mostly they were wallpapered. One room was covered in a bright yellow, sixties, psychedelic swirl, another in a plasticky representation of wood paneling, another in dull arrangements of brown-tinted apples and pears. Our bedroom had the most bearable pattern—a delicate one of bluebells and intertwining vines. I wouldn't have wanted it in my own room at home, but at least it didn't give me the shakes like the yellow room or depress me like the rotting-fruit room.

The main decorations were old, framed maps of France, all with creeping yellow stains in the corners from where moisture had gotten under the glass. There was a framed ad for Casio keyboards in the bathroom— one that looked like it was from the mideighties, with a guy in a big orange suit and a mustache with a keyboard tucked under his arm. I spent a lot of time staring at this, trying to figure out why someone had taken the time to remove it from a magazine, frame it, and hang it next to the sink.

Erique loaded up the tiny fridge with food, stacked loaves of bread and warm Orangina and bottled water on the shelf, and then putt-putted off in his car. We looked around for something to do. For entertainment there was a shelfful of French romance novels, detective stories, guidebooks, and history books—all in the early stages of pungent old-book smell. There were also some old board games and a television with antennae and no cable that got only one station, which showed only American cartoons dubbed into French, mostly Bob l'éponge, who lived in a pineapple under the sea.

To be fair to the place, I think most French people who rented it rolled up with their own bikes and kayaks and Casio keyboards or whatever else they needed. Claude had indicated he would be bringing all these things just as soon as he could get here, so all we had to do was "relax"—which, as everyone knows, is another way of saying "sit around and wait and feel the creeping hand of time run its fingers up your back." I couldn't stand it, all woody and quiet and smelling of rosemary and thyme. It was like being in a spice rack.

We walked around outside, but the smallness of the frogs freaked Marylou out a lot, mostly because they kept jumping across the path when we were least expecting it, and she stepped on one by accident, and she went through all five stages of grief about it. Marylou is famous for her squeamishness and her nonviolent nature. Spiders, silverfish, roaches, even flies . . . she's helpless against them. At home she would make someone else, often me, come and deal with the problem. So killing a frog almost did her in. The rest of the afternoon was spent calming her down. That night we had dinner, read all the books we'd brought, and waited.

Two days went by like this. Erique came every afternoon and brought us delicious and rustic-looking French groceries and looked at us helplessly, sometimes pointing at the clock or shaking a bottle of milk in a meaningful way. We never had any idea what he was trying to say. The only time we could ever understand was when he showed us a tiny dead scorpion, laughed, then took off his shoe, and shook it. This baffled us at first, but since he did it every time he left us, we slowly began to realize that we had to shake out our shoes before we stepped into them because they might be filled with scorpions.

We were safe and well fed and generally looked after, but slowly going crazy. Or so Marylou thought, from the number of times she diagnosed me from the rocking chair in our bedroom. Over those days and nights I had: generalized anxiety disorder, ADHD, body dysmorphic disorder, adjustment disorder, and borderline kleptomania (because I kept using her brush).

And then I was depressed. Now you're all caught up. This was day three.

"You aren't enjoying this either," I said. "So I guess either we're both abnormal or we're both depressed. And why'd you bring that with you? That's not exactly vacation reading."

"It is if you want a four point oh. And what else is there to do?"

She had a good point. I was staring at an issue of French *Vogue* from 1984. I mean, it was fun looking at the big hair, but you can only do that for so long. I set it aside and picked up the useless little pay-as-you-go French cell phone Claude had gotten us (because our American ones didn't work right and would have cost about a million dollars a second if they had).

"Maybe it's the house that's messing up the phone," I said, not believing that for a second. The last time I had seen a signal, we were at the train station, ten or more miles away. "There's got to be *somewhere* around here where a cell phone works. I have to find out."

"Feel free," Marylou said, flicking her hand but not looking up. "Go try."

"Doesn't this freak you out at all?" I said. "Three days. He said it would take him, like, one."

"He never said that. He said he'd be here as soon as he could. He has someone bringing us food twice a day— really good food—and we're in a beautiful house. . . ."

"Beautiful?" I repeated.

". . . we're in a house in the middle of the French countryside. It's important to try to adapt to a different way of life, a different pace. Quiet is good."

I shuddered.

"I hate quiet," I said.

She flipped a page, to whatever disorder it is that is characterized by a hatred of being in quiet, remote places.

"Why don't you come?" I asked.

"Frogs," she said. "I'm fine here."

I went outside and sat down on the path with my legs out in front of me and let the little frogs jump over my ankles. They really seemed to like this. My ankles were clearly the best thing that had happened in tiny frog land for a while. It felt better to be outside at least and out of the airless house. I started walking back to the road. It was a pretty view, no question. But even the prettiest view will wear on your nerves if you're feeling very cut off and bored and uncertain about what the hell is going on. So while I appreciated the soft yellow sunlight spread out over the white hills around us, the bright stripes of purple lavender crops, and the heady smell of pine . . . what I *wanted* to see were bars in my cell phone display.

I walked for at least two miles, with nothing but the beautiful view to keep me company. No people, no signal. I passed through an olive orchard, the trees heavy with fruit. I saw some fuzzy little animal scamper across the path. Otherwise, nothing.

I finally came to a small red cottage, one with an actual person milling around in front of it. I say milling because that's really what he was doing. I'd never seen real *milling* before. Done right, real milling has a shambling quality to it, a true aimlessness that can be felt by any spectator. He was circling the lawn at the front of the house.

The miller was nice enough looking, in his twenties or thirties, with longish, artsy hair. He was covered in dirt, on his knees and shorts and hands, like he'd just been working in the garden. There was a plastic basketful of large tomatoes, peppers, and eggplants sitting on the stone front step. He had a look of total confusion on his face, and a nervous way of smoking, like he just couldn't get enough nicotine and had to suck in quick, greedy gulps. He saw me, blinked a few times, waved stiffly, and said *bonjour*. I said *bonjour* back . . . but when he started speaking rapid-fire French, I shook my head and came closer.

"Sorry," I said. "I don't speak—"

"Oh," he said quickly. "You are English? American?"

"American," I said.

The man's English was perfect, though he was clearly French. His accent was light—it just tweaked the ends of his words.

"My dog," he said. "I'm looking for my dog. He often

goes out hunting rabbits, but he has been gone for hours now. Have you seen a dog?"

"No," I said. "I'm sorry."

He bit his lower lip thoughtfully and stared at the trees again.

"I am afraid he may have gotten stuck in a hole or hurt," he said. "I call and call, but he does not come."

He sucked the last of the cigarette down to the butt and dropped it to the grass, still burning. It snuffed itself out.

"You are visiting?" he said.

"Yeah . . . my sister and I . . . we're at the cottage up the road, and our cousin—"

"I know the cottage," he said.

"I'm trying to make a phone call. Our cell phones don't work out here. No reception."

"Cell phones? Ah . . . mobiles. Yes, they do not work here. I'm sorry. I have no other phone. My name is Henri. And yours?"

"Char—" Everyone calls me Charlie. But it seemed like I should use my real name in France, to forge my new, Frenchier identity. "—lotte."

"Charlotte. But you are thirsty? It is very warm. Would you like a drink?"

He waved me indoors without waiting for my answer, picking up the basket as we went inside.

"Did you grow those?" I asked.

He looked down at the basket. It seemed like he had forgotten he was holding it.

"Yes," he said distractedly. "We have a very good garden."

The door opened directly into a large farmhouse kitchen with a rough-hewn wood floor, dried bundles of herbs hanging from the ceiling, and a huge red stove with massive, flat burners covered by heavy lids. The basket went onto the table.

"I have lemonade," he said. "It is very nice."

I thanked him, and he poured me a glass. It was certainly very authentic—so tart that I almost started weeping. But I felt like I had to get through it somehow, just to be polite.

"You are here with your family?" he asked.

Again, he said it vacantly, picking up another cigarette from the pack on the table, lighting it, and sucking it quickly.

"Just my sister, Marylou," I reminded him. "Well, actually Marie-Louise."

Henri's eyes came fully into focus, like he was seeing me for the first time. He slowed down on the smoking, taking an easy drag and setting the cigarette down in an ashtray.

"Your names are quite funny," he said. "Very historical."

"They are?"

"Do you know much about the French Revolution?" he asked.

"A little," I said. And by "a little," I meant almost nothing, but it looked like he was prepared to do most of the talking, so I was okay.

"Well, as I am sure you know, the people overthrew the king and queen and killed off most of the aristocracy. There was a period called the Terror, where thousands of people were killed. Then there was the Law of Suspects. It meant that any citizen determined to be an enemy of the people could be locked up at once or executed. I suppose now we would call them terrorists. . . . Anyone could be accused. Anyone could be killed. Anyone could be capable."

I was nodding away, wondering where this was heading, but mostly I was trying to figure out how to drink the lemonade without getting it on the part of my tongue that really reacted to the sourness.

"Marie-Louise was the name of the Princesse de Lamballe, the confidant of Marie Antoinette. She was killed in the September Massacres in 1792. Do you know what they did to her?"

"No," I said.

"They dragged her from the prison at La Force. A mob descended on her, ripping her to shreds. They sliced her head from her body and took it to a hairdresser to have it . . . how would you say it . . . styled? Then they put it on a pike and carried it to Marie Antoinette's window and stuck it inside, like a puppet. And Charlotte . . . that is the name of the most famous murderess in all of France. Charlotte Corday. She stabbed Jean-Paul Marat in the bathtub. There is a very famous painting of this."

"Right," I said. "But our names are kind of common."

"They are, of course. This is true."

He lit up another cigarette, and I noticed that Henri was a bit on the twitchy side. He had to work his way through four matches before he could get it lit. I sort of knew what he was talking about, but now I was ready for him to be done. This was maybe more than I had bargained for, conversation-wise, and I was done with the lemonade. I still had no cell phone signal, and I was going to have to hurry back if I was going to make it on time for Bob l'éponge.

"This is just French history," he said. "You learn it as a child. But it has always proved a point to me: anyone is capable of murder. Anyone. Many in the revolution said they killed to be free, but this does not explain the mobs. . . . The people who raided the houses, who dragged screaming people to the streets and tore their flesh, the washerwomen who cried for blood at the guillotine. Completely normal people, average citizens. The revolutionary spirit, it was called. It was never the revolutionary spirit. It was the spirit of murder. It is in France, it is everywhere. . . ."

There was something officially weird about Henri now, at least to me. Maybe this was just a French way of being friendly: a little story about famous mass murders of the past to break the ice. He went on and on about various atrocities until I felt I simply had to bring a halt to the proceedings.

"Would you mind if I used your bathroom?" I asked as he took a breath between sentences.

This request caught Henri off guard for a moment, and he fumbled with his cigarette a little.

"Yes . . . of course. The toilet is at the top of the stairs."

Henri's house was much nicer than ours, but that made sense, as he actually lived there. The living room was very neat. There was no television in there—just a lot of bookcases, some camera equipment, a massive printer, and what seemed to be a nice stereo. The walls were covered in artsy photographs: some of the landscape and some of Henri and a woman, who I presumed was his wife. In one, near the top of the stairs, the woman was completely naked . . . but it was very tasteful and French and kind of touching. There were piles of books absolutely everywhere and a few dog toys on the floor.

The bathroom was right at the top of the steps, as he said. It was a stark room with blue tiles. There were no towels, no bath mat, no curtains, no toilet paper, no shower curtain—nothing soft. No soap, even. It was as if no one lived here, no one used this bathroom at all.

When I came back downstairs, Henri was standing in the wide-open doorway. A wind had kicked up, and the big red door banged away on the hinges into the face of the house. The wind whipped into the hall and sent things fluttering all over the place. None of this seemed to bother Henri.

"A storm, I think," he said. "I think tonight. Can I offer you something to eat?"

"No," I said quickly. "I should get back. My sister . . . she'll worry."

"Ah, yes. Your sister."

"The pictures are really nice," I said. "Is that your wife?"

He looked as if he had absolutely no idea what I was talking about.

"The pictures along the stairs," I said, pointing back at the dozen or more framed prints.

"My wife," he repeated. "Yes. My wife."

"We'll be around for a while," I said, slipping past him and out the door. "And I'll keep an eye out for a lost dog."

I walked back toward our house quickly, wanting to put as much distance between Henri and me as possible. The wind blew like hell the whole way back, throwing dirt and pollen in my eyes. I was a half-blind wheezing mess when I got back to our bedroom, where Marylou was in the same exact position, her tiny feet tucked up on the chair. She had closed the heavy blue shutters on the bedroom window to block out the wind, so now the room was fairly dark, lit only by an ancient lamp in the corner.

"People around here are weird," I said.

Marylou looked up from *The Big Book of Crazy.*

"Define weird," she said.

"Weird as in I passed one house on the way, and the guy in it was just standing around like a zombie looking for his dog, and all he talked about was the French Revolution and the spirit of murder and something about some suspect law. He was very creepy. He didn't have anything in his bathroom—"

"Charlie," she said, putting her thumb in her book and closing it. "I thought you stopped that."

"I'm serious."

But it was clear that she didn't believe me.

"We should just go back to Paris," I said. "Get back to town, take the same train we came in on. This place sucks."

"Except that Claude's probably on his way here. So we'd get there and have nowhere to go. Didn't you have any luck with the phone?"

I shook my head.

"Well, Erique brought the groceries while you were out. We should eat, I guess."

Erique had brought delicious food for us—roast

chicken, bread, tomatoes, and soft cheese full of lavender. There was yet more warm Orangina. The wind battered the house as Marylou set our Hobbit-y table with the heavy blue-and-white plates from the cupboard. She closed the kitchen shutters as well, and the room went dark. I sat on one of the benches, staring at the pattern of knots and ridges in the wood of the table.

"Come on," she said. "Eat. It's not that bad here. Try this."

She tore off some of the chicken with a fork and cut me a hunk of the cheese and bread. It was all delicious— the crisp chicken studded with thyme, the cheese with the pretty purple flecks of lavender. I think I should have felt content and French, safe and snug inside, with the wind whistling outside. But I didn't. I felt just slightly sick.

"What is with you?" she asked.

"It was that guy and his weird-ass story."

"All right," she said, spreading cheese thick on a piece of bread. "What did he say that freaked you out so much?"

So I told her everything I could remember about Henri's story, going to great lengths to stick to the facts exactly as I'd heard them. When I finished, Marylou just shook her head.

"So he likes history," she said. "And he's a little morbid. You can't just write him off as crazy, Charlie."

"That's not the word we like to use," I corrected her.

Marylou laughed at this. I felt a little better once I'd gotten the story out. The wind didn't seem so blustery. I took a big piece of chicken, and we talked about other things for a while, like the fact that Marylou had found a set of Ping-Pong paddles and balls when I was gone and how we could convert our table into a Ping-Pong paradise. We were just finishing up when we were startled by a knock at the door. Marylou jumped to answer it.

It wasn't Claude, as we'd both been hoping. The news was actually a bit better than that. It was a guy, maybe Marylou's age. He was tall and lanky, with dark curly hair cut short but uneven. He was wearing a threadbare Led Zeppelin T-shirt and ragged jeans chopped off at the knee. He had a sprig of green something or other in his hair, something off one of the many forms of plant life around us. And he was sweating profusely. All of that aside, he was pretty good looking. Well, very, actually.

He opened his mouth to speak, but I got there first, just to get it out of the way.

"Sorry," I said. "We don't speak French."

"My English is so-so," he said, coming into the room shyly and looking around our little Shire kitchen. "I am Gerard. I live in the village. I saw you earlier, walking the path. I thought I would come, say hello."

We gazed at him stupidly. Turns out, if you're stuck in a French cabin for days on end and a guy shows up, you basically lose your mind. Socials skills right out the window.

"Hello," Marylou finally said. "Do you want . . . um . . . some chicken? Or cheese or . . ."

She pointed at the picked-apart chicken carcass on the table and the mostly eaten cheese and the remains of the bread.

"A drink!" I said, remembering the earlier hospitality. "We have Orangina!"

"A drink. Thank you."

I poured Gerard some Orangina, and he sat at the table with us. He looked down at the glass shyly. He was a strapping boy, the kind who looked like he had been raised in these glorious fields, developing strong muscles through cheese-rolling or whatever it was you did when you were a tall French guy who grew up in a lovely village in the middle of nowhere.

"You are?" he asked.

"I'm Charlie. Charlotte."

"Charlie Charlotte?"

"Either one," I mumbled.

"And I'm Marylou," my sister added. She had seen my fumble, and she wasn't going the French-name route.

"What are you doing 'ere?" he asked.

I got in ahead of Marylou and started telling Gerard the story of Mr. 56E, Claude, the little suits of armor, Erique, the tiny frogs, all the way through Henri and his tale of woe, doom, and weirdness. This last bit seemed to catch Gerard's attention, because he looked up at me the entire time I was talking, his bright brown eyes looking right into mine.

"Henri likes 'istory," he said, but he certainly didn't sound happy about it. I gathered Henri made a habit of talking death and mayhem and history to anyone who got near. Gerard just had that look on his face like he'd heard it all before.

"What do you do?" Marylou asked.

"I go to university in Lyon. I study psychology."

Oh, the joy on Marylou's face. A kindred spirit. She started rambling on about all the good times she'd had in the psych lab tormenting other students for eight dollars an hour. Gerard nodded and occasionally added a comment. I gathered that he was nineteen, had been at university for a year, and wasn't as excited about being a psych major as Marylou. (No one could be, really.) He listened for a good solid hour, but I noticed that he looked at me a lot more than at Marylou.

Which was a bit odd. I just figured that Gerard would be more interested in the one that seemed a little older, saner, and into his subject, but this wasn't the case. Every time Marylou looked away, his eyes met mine with definite interest, and I would twitch a little in excitement. I didn't mind France *at all* with

Gerard in the picture.

"This *DS* . . . *DS* . . ." he said in response to something Marylou was saying.

"The *DSM-IV*," she said.

"Yes. I would very much like to see eet. You say you have eet?"

"Sure!" Marylou was out of her seat in a shot and up the steps to our room. The moment she left, Gerard leaned across the table, coming close to my face.

"Listen to me," he said. "Eef you want to live, eef you love your sister, follow me now."

"What?"

But with that he grabbed my phone and ran.

Okay, so. You're me. You're sitting there with one of the most beautiful guys you've ever seen. And he asks you if you want to live. And he steals your phone. And says you have to follow.

You follow him, right? Because what else are you going to do?

Right?

Maybe not everyone would have done that. I think some people would have immediately bolted the door behind him and started screaming. If I had been like you, if you're one of those people, this story would have turned out a lot differently.

But I went tearing down the path after him, screaming his name. Gerard was fast, and tall, with much longer legs. He quickly outpaced me. I followed him all the way down to the dirt road, where he made a sharp turn, then he headed into the trees. I followed.

Then he was gone. I was just standing in the middle of the woods.

"I am not going to hurt you," Gerard said.

He stepped out from a tree behind me. I backed up, finally realizing that following a thief into the middle of nowhere is a really dumb move.

"Oh," I said.

"This is important, Charlie," he said, stepping closer. "Did you tell your sister the story? The one Henri told you. Did you repeat eet?"

This was the last thing I was expecting to hear, and probably not the kind of thing a person who plans on attacking you says.

"What?"

"You must tell me, Charlie! Did you tell her the story? About the Law of Suspects?"

"Story?" I repeated. "That stupid story Henri told me? Yes! I told her!"

This hit him like a blow. All the muscles in his face seemed to go lax and he fell back against a tree and looked up into the branches in despair. He exhaled once, very slowly, and looked back at me.

"I'm showing you something," he said. "You will not like eet. But you need to see eet to understand what is going on."

He pulled his messenger bag from around his shoulders. From it he removed what appeared to be some trash. Just a bundle of plastic shopping bags. He gave them a shake, and something plopped out onto the path. Something small, like a bird. A dead one.

And I remember thinking, *Why the hell is he carrying around a dead bird?* So my brain kept working on the problem, and eventually it decided that the thing on the path was not a bird. So that was the good news. The bad news was . . .

It was a hand.

Unattached to a body.

A bluish white, bloodless, dismembered hand—cut very neatly about the spot where you'd wear a watch. It was very dirty. It was a smallish hand, but maybe all hands look small when they're . . . disconnected.

For a moment I felt nothing at all, then I got very giddy. I cycled through a lot of emotions, in fact. There was a high, floaty feeling in my head. I laughed. I coughed. I stumbled and went down on all fours.

"I found eet at Henri's house," he said, as if my reaction was exactly what he had been expecting. "Eet was 'alf-buried in the garden by the *aubergines.* Something dug eet up and left eet exposed. I believe this is Henri's wife. Well, 'er hand. The rest of her . . . I think is also there. Now you must listen to me. Your life is depending on eet."

I put my face against the dirt, accidentally sniffing some of it up my nose. I think I was breathing very fast. It smelled mushroomy up this close.

"Charlie," Gerard said, "you may feel sick but this is not the time. . . ."

"It's not?"

I was laughing again and snorting more dirt. He hoisted me up under my arms and got me to my feet.

"Police," I mumbled.

"We do not have time," he said, backing me against a tree and letting me get myself balanced. "Now you must listen, and you must try to understand. We cannot help this person. . . ."

He pointed at the hand, which was still just flopped there, palm up, and taking in our conversation in a passive, disembodied-hand kind of way.

"But we can save you. And your sister. Either one of you could be infected. You could have passed eet to her."

"What . . . are . . . you . . . talking . . . about?"

"This is my fault," he said mournfully. "I must fix this."

Gerard picked up a stick and used it to push the plastic over the hand a little, so that I would stop staring at it. He tipped my chin up to look him in the eye.

"Three weeks ago," he began, "a very famous psychologist died in a car crash along with his wife. He left his library and papers to my university. Thousands of books and papers. I am one of five students asked to go through the papers, read them, sort them. I read through a dozen boxes, maybe more. A few days ago I came home to stay with my cousin for a visit. I was allowed to bring some papers with me. I read them on the train. Many of them were very boring, but then, I find a bundle of papers that looked very old. Attached to them is a note in the psychologist's handwriting that says, 'Do not read.' So I read them. Or most of them. Eet seems that he was studying the murder impulse—how normal people can murder."

I almost laughed and almost said, "Normal isn't a word we like to use." But I was pretty sure that if I tried to talk, I would throw up.

"This psychologist," Gerard went on, "he was a great man, but as he got older, he started to study things many find ridiculous, very unusual areas of psychology. These notes of his talked of a story that made people kill once they heard eet. The story was about the revolution, about the spirit of murder. About the Law of Suspects. Once you hear eet, you will kill someone close to you before the next morning. The papers went on to say that only one person is . . . infected . . . at a time. Like a curse. Once the person murders, they are compelled to tell the story to someone else, then they kill themselves.

"A copy of this deadly story was attached, along with many notes of warning. There was no indication that he had read eet. In fact, eet seemed he had not. He had simply located the last known copy and kept eet. An academic impulse. You cannot get rid of an important document, no matter how dangerous. The notes indicated that eet was in a letter dated 1804. Eet had been lost for many, many years, but he had uncovered eet and wished he hadn't. I did not take eet seriously. Eet is unscientific. Ridiculous. So I stopped reading and fell asleep."

At this, he shook his head miserably.

"When I got to my cousin's, I told her the story over a coffee. She laughed and asked to see the papers. They are not secret, so I showed her. That night I went out with friends. I stayed out very late. I came in and went right to sleep. . . ."

It was obviously hard for Gerard to say these things. But I had no doubt that they were true. Liars are good at seeing the truth. The color had gone from his face and he was grabbing at his hair. The shock caused by the hand deepened into dread, a dread that sank into my bones and made me unable to move.

"The next morning the house was quiet. My cousin and her husband made no noise. After some time I was worried. So I opened the bedroom door. That is when I found her husband. He had been stabbed with a corkscrew, deep into the ear. My cousin was in the closet. She had hung herself with the . . . the tie . . . from around the waist of her dressing gown. This was three days ago."

I remembered the police car and the ambulance. That must have been the house. We had gone right past it and had no idea.

"The police thought she had perhaps gone insane, gone into a jealous rage, but I knew my cousin. There was nothing wrong with her until she read that story. I do not know how this works or why. The Law of Suspects story is real, and I brought eet back by bringing those papers here. I wasn't able to get back into the house for a day, but when I did . . . the papers were nowhere. I asked the police eef they had taken them, but they had not. I remembered that the psychologist claimed the story would be passed on before death. I thought my cousin had posted the papers to someone. For the last two days I have watched her friends. I saw Henri in the village this morning, picking up some post. Later I went along to his house. I saw you there. I saw him fresh from the garden, acting very strange. I went to the garden while you were inside with him. I found this. . . ."

He gestured toward the plastic-covered hand.

"I have not seen his wife. Have you?"

"No," I said, managing to find my voice. "He said he was looking for his dog."

"His dog," he said, nodding. "Yes. That makes sense. The dog was always with his wife. When he attacked her, I imagine the dog tried to stop him. The dog must also be dead."

"So you're saying," I said, "that Henri is infected by some *story in a letter*, and he killed his wife."

"I do not want to believe eet myself. But my cousin and her husband are dead. And Henri has just buried a body in his garden. And he has told you a story exactly as I described. The next steps are clear. Henri will die, and either you or your sister will be infected. It can only be one. Before the night is over, one will kill the other, and then commit suicide."

This was not possible. None of it was possible. But there was a hand. And I remembered how I felt after Henri spoke to me. It wasn't right. It wasn't *normal*. Something had happened.

"According to his notes," he said, "there is a way. There *have* been cases where people have been spared because they went to safety, or were alone. You must both put yourself in a place where you cannot hurt anyone."

A silence fell between us. From far away, I heard Marylou calling for me. This brought me back to the reality of being in the woods with Gerard and the hand.

"Please, Charlie," he begged, getting up. "Do not

go back. Look. I have . . . I have water and food. Here. Enough for one night."

More things were produced from the bag. A bottle of water. Some candy bars. A small flashlight. He set the food on the ground and pressed the flashlight into my hand.

"Henri knows what he has done. He has passed the story on. His time is ending. Eef you go now, eef you can get through until morning, then you will be fine. You simply need to be isolated. Take these things and spend the night out here, as far from the house as you can get. As far from the village. You get lost."

"Oh," I said, laughing now. "I see. I get lost in the woods for the night. Sounds great, Gerard. Sounds like a plan. And why did you have to tell this to me out here?"

"Your sister would not believe me," he said simply. "But I felt you would. I hope you do."

The sky had gotten darker and the air soupier. The storm Henri had promised earlier was sitting on top of us, waiting to erupt. I stared at the water and the candy. Food that had been in a bag with a severed hand.

"You're right about one thing," I said. "We need to get out of here."

I turned and started walking back. I heard Gerard calling to me, pleading. But I kept going. He did not follow me.

As I pushed back through the branches, following the sound of Marylou's voice to the house, I assessed my situation. That it was a real hand, I was sure. That was the big thing here. Someone was dead. And Henri's bare bathroom, stripped of anything that might . . . soak up blood. Towels and paper. If I was going to cut up a body, I'd do it in a tub. Then I'd wash the tub and bleach it. Then I'd get rid of everything else. Yes, that made sense. So Gerard had had a trauma and thought this was all based on some story. Grief and guilt had confused him. But there was still a danger here, and that danger was Henri. Henri knew where we lived. He knew our phones didn't work. He knew we were alone. Which meant that I had to convince Marylou that we needed to get out *right now.*

Everything looked blurry and odd. I started to run, paying no attention to the tiny frogs that might be under my feet, feeling like I was bouncing high with each step. The slowly darkening sky looked like one of the landscapes that Van Gogh used to paint here: swirly clouds against a bright palette of sunset colors. The view of the house throbbed in time with my pulse. Marylou was waiting for me at the open door, looking furious, still holding her trusty *DSM-IV.*

"There you are!" she said. "I left for two minutes and you were gone! What the hell is going on?"

I pushed her inside and bolted the door behind me.

"What's wrong?" she asked as I slumped on one of the kitchen benches. "Charlie, you look sick. You're so pale."

She was *not* going to believe the hand. Not, not, not going to believe it. It would take something else, something more plausible. It would take a lie. A megaton of a lie.

I had one in a second.

"Gerard," I said. "That guy. He's nuts. He stole my phone, and he ran out. I chased him, and he tried to attack me. I just barely got away. He's still out there. We have to get out of here."

"What?" she said, coming to sit by me and putting an arm around my shoulders. "Charlie . . . did he hurt you?"

"I'm fine. I hit him. With this." I held up the flashlight. "I don't know what he was going to do with it, but I got it off of him and I hit him with it. I whacked him in the head, hard, and he kind of ran off. Now we have to get out, get to the village, and get help. *This is not a lie.* Look at me."

I could see Marylou testing out the plausibility of my story in her head. I have to say, I gave a magnificent performance. What I was saying wasn't exactly true, but the sentiment behind it certainly was. My fear was real. And I had his flashlight. And she had probably seen him running. There was a lot to back up my story.

Marylou got up and paced the kitchen while she weighed the facts. I saw acceptance flash over her face.

"How old do you think he was?" she asked. "Eighteen? Nineteen? It's common for people that age to experience a minor psychotic break."

"That's reassuring," I said, swallowing hard.

"If he's out there, we need to stay in here. We need to lock everything."

"No," I countered quickly. "He said he'd come back. He said he'd get in. This is our only shot. If we go right now, we could get to town before he catches up with us."

Marylou stepped back from the bench and put her hands on her hips, looking worriedly around the room.

"Okay," she said. "Okay. Here."

She went to the hooks at the back of the kitchen and pulled down two of the heavy green rain slickers that were hanging there.

"Put that on," she said, dropping one of the slickers on the table. "It's going to rain."

She rattled around in one of the kitchen drawers and produced a heavy carving knife, which she passed to me.

"Put this in something," she said.

"What's this for?"

"Protection. I'm going to close the rest of the shutters upstairs. You do the ones down here."

Up the stairs she went. I went into the other two

rooms and shut the shutters against nothing, then put on my slicker.

"I found this too," she said, running back down the stairs. It was a piece of heavy pipe, about a foot long, that looked like a section of something much larger. "If he comes near us, this will knock him out."

My sister was surprisingly good with the improvised weaponry, especially for someone who couldn't even handle a spider. If Gerard was watching, I prayed that he just avoided us.

The air tasted moist, and everything smelled deeply of earth and wet lavender. It was a strange sky, everything going soft and fuzzy in the greenish diffused light. The frogs were out in full froggy force, and we practically had to dance down the path to avoid them. Aside from the wildly chirping cicadas, there was no noise except our feet on the gravel. The trees and heavy air seemed to soak up and muffle all other noise.

We saw no one on our walk. Marylou had the pipe at the ready the entire time. It started to rain after the first mile or so. It came down hard, making a deafening racket on the hoods of the heavy slickers. The pits in the road filled with water and were impossible to see, so we kept tripping into them.

The rain had one advantage, though. It made visibility poor. When we got to Henri's cottage, it was easy to block Marylou's field of vision and keep her looking the other way so she couldn't spot it through the trees. We got past it, about another quarter mile or so, before my illusions of safety were shattered. We found him standing in the road, staring at nothing. Henri raised a hand in distracted greeting. He didn't seem to notice the pounding rain. A cigarette disintegrated in his hand.

"My dog," he said loudly. "I cannot find my dog."

There was nothing I could do. Marylou was instantly rambling our dilemma at Henri, who didn't seem to understand a word of it, but he pointed back toward his house. Marylou followed. So I did too.

It was humid in the kitchen now. Henri had been cutting onions. Loads of them. They were piled on the counter, a dozen or so. The cutting board on the table was piled high with them, sliced and chopped, an overflowing bowl next to it as well.

"I am making soup," he said tonelessly. "Onion soup."

A small television and DVD player sat on the end of the table, and *Mission: Impossible* (in French of course) was on, and Tom Cruise was doing his little Tom Cruise run.

"We need to call the police," Marylou said. "A guy came to our cottage today. What was his name? Ger . . . Gerald?"

I made no effort to correct her, but it was a small village and Henri knew who she meant.

"There is a *Gerard*," he said.

"That's him," Marylou said, nodding. "Kind of tall? Dark curly hair?"

"That sounds like Gerard."

Henri didn't seem too concerned about all of this. He pulled a bulb of garlic from a rope hanging in the corner and sat down at his cutting board. He took a moment to put a fresh cigarette in his mouth but didn't light it. Then he picked up the enormous knife. I reached for Marylou to pull her back, but he merely gave the garlic a massive thwack with the side of the knife to break it into cloves.

"My mother would cook the onions for hours," he said. "In two bottles of wine. She would add them slowly, drip by drip."

Smack, smack, smack. He whacked each clove of garlic, shattering the papery skin and breaking it off with his fingers. Marylou looked at me sideways and tried again. The heat and humid stench of onions in the room took my breath away.

"A phone," she said. "We need to call the police. He attacked Charlie."

"He attacked you?" Henri asked, not sounding overly concerned. "This surprises me."

"He did," Marylou assured him, thus spreading my lie.

"Well, he cannot hurt you here. Sit down. It will be fine here. You are safe here. My wife . . . but she is not here right now."

There was a strange omission in the sentence.

"Do you know this movie?" he asked, pointing the onion-sticky knife at the screen. "It is very American, but I enjoy it. Watch."

"The police," Marylou said again.

Henri went right on chopping. I had to do something— look around for a phone, a computer, something. Marylou had stashed the pipe under her slicker. If anything went wrong, hopefully she would use it.

"The bathroom," I said, falling back on my old excuse. "Could I . . ."

He waved the knife as permission.

In the dark, knowing what I knew now . . . nothing was more horrible than those dark steps, the dozen photos of Henri's wife. I have never felt so frightened. So alone. So doomed.

So when I got to the top of the steps and Gerard clapped his hand over my mouth and pulled me into the bathroom, I was actually quite relieved. His other arm wrapped around my body, holding me still. He leaned in very close to me, so close that I could feel his warmth and smell the light smell of sweat and the outdoors and feel his breath on my ear.

"I followed you here," he said very quietly. "I climbed up a tree and came in through the window. I weel let you go. Do not scream. I trust you not to scream."

He released my mouth and then me.

"Why did you say I attacked you?" he asked.

"I had to say something," I whispered to him. "Something to get Marylou to leave."

Gerard looked a bit hurt but nodded.

"You should never have come here. . . ."

"It was Marylou," I said.

"Henri has a car. I don't know where the keys are. When you go downstairs, you find the keys, and you take them. And then you put your sister in the car and drive out of here. You are all right as long as Henri is alive. Get to safety. Get to the police—"

"You want me to *steal his car*?"

"Eet is better than the alternative. Do what I say this time. Please."

I don't know why I was listening to Gerard. Of the two people involved in this, he was considerably weirder. All Henri had done was tell us history and make soup. Gerard won the crazy race by a mile, on the face of things, but still . . . I believed him. I believed that Henri had done something very, very terrible and that we were in a lot of danger.

"Marylou is *not* going to come along if I steal a car," I said, steadying myself against the wall.

"No," he said with a nod. "She will have to be taken unwillingly. Knock her out. I can help you with that. I will wait outside, and when you come out with the keys, I will punch her. Eet will be very quick. She will feel eet later, but eet is better than the alternative."

Here he was with "the alternative" again, all the while casually talking about creeping out of the darkness and punching my sister in the face.

"What?" I said.

"I know how to do eet."

"How?"

"I was a lifeguard," he said plainly. "You learn to do this when people struggle in the water. You need to hit the jaw. Getting punched is—"

"I know," I said. Clearly the phrase "better than the alternative" was one Gerard had mastered in his English lessons. Not that I knew what he meant. "Isn't there another way? And are you saying that this alternative—"

"You do not have time to wait. Go back down there and look for the keys and—"

Before he could say any more, the door swung open, and Henri stood there, with a small hunting rifle in his hands.

"*Bonsoir*, Gerard," he said.

Henri moved us both down to the kitchen. His gun was on Gerard the entire time, but I felt pretty certain that he wouldn't have particularly objected to using it on me. When we got down there, he made Gerard sit in a chair, and politely asked Marylou to tie him to it with a spool of rope he had by the door: ankles and wrists.

"You have to call the police," Marylou said, for what had to be the tenth time.

"We must secure him first," he said. "Please make sure that it is tight."

Marylou didn't look happy, but she got down on her knees behind Gerard and tied him up, knotting the rope over and over. Gerard winced but never once took his eyes from Henri's face.

"So why don't we take your car into town?" Gerard asked. "You want to turn me in to the police, go ahead."

"No petrol. I was going to walk and get some more in the morning. Now . . ."

For a moment he seemed distracted by the sight of Tom Cruise on his tiny television, but soon he refocused on the situation at hand.

"You've been giving these girls some trouble," he said. "You've snuck into my house. What exactly are you doing, Gerard?"

"Open my bag and see."

Henri pulled Gerard's ragged messenger bag closer with his foot, bent and pulled open the snap with one hand, and dumped the contents to the floor. The candy bars and water bottles were in there; Gerard must have picked them back up. There was also a utility blade.

"What is this?" Henri said, holding it up.

"Well," I said quickly, "we have a knife too."

"Charlie!" Marylou yelled, wheeling around to stare at me.

"Do you?" Henri asked, sounding profoundly unconcerned.

"Because of him," Marylou said, pointing at Gerard. "We brought it for protection."

I tried to communicate "We would not have stabbed you, or at least I wouldn't have" with my eyes, but that seemed a hard sentiment to get across. I'm not even sure if Gerard cared at this point. We were all armed to the teeth, but Henri was the *most* armed, and Gerard was tied to a chair, so the knife count was moot.

Anyway, there was a much bigger problem in that bag, and Henri was just getting to it. He had reached the bundle of plastic bags and was unraveling them with a series of sharp shakes.

Then the hand hit the floor. Gerard and I knew what it was, but Henri and Marylou had to take a better look.

"Is that a dead bird?" Marylou asked, grimacing.

"It doesn't look like a bird," Henri said grimly. He figured it out fairly quickly, I think. It took Marylou another moment, and then she screamed. In my ear.

"I found that in the garden, just outside of this house," Gerard said. "Did the dog dig eet up, Henri? Or was eet some other animal? Did the dog try to stop you when you killed your wife? Did you even know what you were doing? Where is your wife, Henri? *Where is your wife?*"

The silence that followed had a horrible, sucking quality to it. Marylou's gasps were snuffed out in a moment. The air was heavy with the onion sting, and the tension made it suddenly, painfully hot.

Henri picked up the remote control and switched off the television.

"I think it is safer if you two stay upstairs," Henri said, mostly to Marylou. "There is a good lock on the front bedroom door. Take your sister and go there."

"I'm not leaving," I heard myself say. I was completely convinced that if we walked away, Henri would kill Gerard. There was no way I was leaving him bound and helpless.

"Go," Henri said. And there was a note in his voice that told me that this is what I *had* to do or he would shoot Gerard right now. I could see Gerard from behind quietly straining at the ropes that bound him. Marylou had me by the arm. Her nails were digging in, and she was crying and saying, "Come on, Charlie; come on, Charlie" over and over. Gerard managed to turn his head enough to look at me. He was afraid. But he nodded, telling me to go. I let Marylou drag me up the steps.

The bedroom was stripped in the same eerie way as the bathroom. There were no sheets, no blankets, no curtains. Marylou was trembling but maintained her poise, pacing the room. I heard muffled voices from downstairs, but it was hard to hear and all in French. It sounded calm, though.

"Marylou," I said. "It's not Gerard. I lied. He never attacked me. I wasn't running from him."

"What?" she said, wheeling around.

"It's too complicated to explain. . . ."

"Try!"

"It was Henri," I snapped. "That hand. It's Henri. . . . It's his wife . . . her hand. Gerard was trying to warn us away. I didn't think you'd believe me so I said he attacked me."

"So you're saying that Henri killed his wife. . . ."

"And probably his dog," I added.

"And Gerard came around to tell us that. Because he knew. Because he found her hand. . . ."

"You *saw* the hand," I said.

"I saw *a* hand. That was in Gerard's bag."

"Well, where do you *think* he got a hand?" I yelled. "They don't *sell* them here. It's not a *kind of meat*."

"*I don't know where he got a hand!* But he had a knife! And you said he attacked you!"

"I just told you I was lying!"

"Oh great!" she screamed. "That's very helpful! Just be quiet a second. I need to think."

The storm beat away at the shutters, clapping them

against the side of the house, providing a horrible rhythm beneath our argument. The mumbles downstairs had stopped. Marylou sat on the edge of the bare mattress and put her head in her hands.

Then we heard the gunshot. And a thump. And nothing. So much adrenaline flooded my system, I felt like I could have broken down the door by running at it headfirst. Which is what I did. Run at it headfirst, I mean, while screaming Gerard's name. Marylou grabbed me and held me back. She held hard too, clawing in with her nails and tossing me back on the bed.

"Charlie!" she screamed, getting in my face. "You are not going down there!"

"Did you hear that?" I yelled back. "He shot Gerard! I told you! Gerard was innocent! He was trying to help us!"

"I don't know what's going on, but we are staying in here!"

"Fine. . . ." I said, backing off by crab-crawling backward on the bed. "Fine. . . ."

She went back to the door to make sure it was secured. Now I knew what Gerard had been saying. There was no time to argue with Marylou. The only way I could get her out of danger was by knocking her out and dragging her out of here—because otherwise we would stay up here, and eventually Henri would come back up those steps with his gun. I looked around for something to hit her with. This was so much harder than you might think. The lamps looked like they would kill her; the hairbrush would just annoy her. It was like Goldilocks: too soft, too hard. . . .

I finally saw a sleek DVD player much like the one downstairs (Henri really liked his DVDs). It was thin and looked light. While she was securing the door, I quietly pulled the cords loose from the wall and the back of the television with a rough tug. In protest the player spit out a disk. I pushed the drawer shut.

How would I do this? Gerard had said the jaw, but that didn't make any sense. It had to be the back of the head.

I weighed the DVD player in my grip. One side felt hollow; the other seemed to contain all the parts. I turned it so the heavier side would be the one I would strike with. My hands were sweating. I wiped each one on my jeans. Marylou turned around.

"Charlie, what are you—"

I hit her across the face—a solid clunk against bone that reverberated through the DVD player. She staggered and screamed but didn't fall. I'd bloodied her—I'm not sure from where. Probably the nose.

"Sorry," I gasped.

I hit her again. On the back of the head as I'd originally intended. She lurched forward to tackle me, and I swung out one more time, baseball-bat style, swinging far back and bringing the player right under her chin with all my might. She dropped to the floor, a thin stream of blood flowing from her nose, cutting across her cheek in a thin stripe. I quickly checked to make sure she was still breathing, then I rolled her under the bed to hide her.

"Sorry," I said again, pushing her as far as I could. I opened a drawer and pulled out some clothes, scattering them around the space to hide her as much as I could. This was bad camouflage, but I was making this up as I went and I defy you to do better if this ever happens to you.

I stayed on my hands and knees for a moment, catching my breath. There was no noise from downstairs. That seemed bad. But there was also no noise on the steps or outside the door.

Marylou had brought her bag with her. I slipped the pipe from it, as well as the knife. I held one in each hand, trying to figure out which one was best for the immediate job. The pipe, probably. I crept to the door and undid the lock. I stood for a moment, pipe ready, in case the knob turned and the door opened.

Nothing. Nothing but my heartbeat. Nothing but my own blood pumping so hard my arms shook.

I reached for the knob, holding it tight, then threw the door open. I did that move from police shows to get to the steps—the one where you jump into doorways ready to swing.

I heard a faint shuffle from downstairs. From the kitchen. Henri was still down there.

I tightened my grip on the pipe and took the steps as gingerly as I could, willing my body to weigh nothing, not to inflict any pressure on the old wood. The shuffling continued in the kitchen, and I tried to move in time with it. Then I was at the kitchen doorway, the smell of onions burning my nose. It smelled like Henri had taken the time to actually put them on the stove. I could hear them sizzling. But no other movement. I readied myself.

And then a hand shot out and grabbed my wrist, making me drop the pipe. I screamed.

"Is okay!" Gerard said.

He was untied, standing there, alone.

"What?" I said, gasping. "What . . ."

And then I saw.

Henri was lying on the floor on his back. His head . . . well, what was left of his head . . . a lot of it was missing. . . . I didn't take a good look. He was dead. There was a massive splatter all over that corner of the room, and the blood ran all around him, funneled through the grooves in the wooden floor. The shotgun was on the table.

"What happened?" I said. I felt hot and faint, and I had to grab the doorway for support.

"He untied me," Gerard said, sounding shocked. "He let me go. And then he shot 'imself. Where is your sister?"

"I knocked her out with a DVD player," I said.

He nodded absently. I stepped around him and had a better look at Henri. He was definitely dead. There was so much blood.

"I think he saw the hand and remembered what he did," Gerard said quietly. "Eet has happened just like the notes said, just like my cousin. Henri has killed himself, and now eet will move."

"Oh," I replied.

The onions popped in the pan. I pulled them off the burner. I couldn't figure out how to turn it off. Gerard came over and lowered one of the heavy covers over it.

"You believe now," he said quietly. "I did not want to either, but once you have seen eet, you know eet is true."

Henri's dead body was on the floor, half a head missing. What had seemed so impossible now seemed utterly plausible. The curse was here.

"Yes," I said. "I believe it now."

"How do you feel?" he asked.

"Fine. I mean, I just beat Marylou over the head. But I didn't kill her. That's good, right? I was careful about that."

This news cheered him. His face perked up a bit.

"That is good, Charlie! That is very good!"

I remembered how Marylou had grabbed the knife and the pipe earlier, how she had fought me just now . . . how all of her instincts had been so murderous.

"It's her," I said. "She's got it. I'm sure of it. She's been acting strange."

Gerard watched me carefully for a moment, examining me for any signs that I might break into a murderous rampage. He looked at Marylou's pipe, which was now on the bench next to the table. Then he smiled, pure relief flooding his features.

"Yes," he said. "Eef you did not kill her when you could, eef she is acting odd . . . yes. I believe you are right. Eet is your sister. We will lock her up then we will all be safe. We will all be safe, Charlie!"

With that he pulled me close. I don't know what it was—maybe the mad excitement—but he kissed me. I mean a passionate, full-on, total-body-contact kiss in the true French fashion, done only as a tall village boy who was massively glad to be alive could kiss.

Which, if you are interested, is pretty good stuff. I was pretty glad to be alive myself, and the moment just swelled in that blood-splattered, onion-reeking kitchen with the rain driving away outside. Gerard paused to laugh, his lips close to mine, then picked me up giddily. I wrapped my legs around his hips for support, and we kissed again.

Neither of us heard Marylou come in, or noticed her quietly pick up the rifle.

"What have you *done*?" she said.

She really didn't look good. The blood had smeared on her face, and there were shadowy bruises all along her jaw and cheek. Her eyes were red and teary, and her teeth were set together.

And we were, you know, making out over a dead body with half a head, so I could see how this was going to be a tricky one.

Gerard lowered me slowly, and I tried to smile. A calm, it's-all-okay-now smile.

"You don't understand. . . ." I said.

"That is the biggest understatement of all time."

Marylou backed up to the doorway and swung the gun between the two of us.

"You killed him," she said to Gerard.

"No," I said quickly. "He killed himself. Because he killed his wife. Just like I said."

"You mean before you beat me over the head?"

She started to laugh—a high, very crazy laugh that could have been an audio sample that played when you opened the *DSM-IV*, like one of those chips in a musical greeting card. It was a fair point. I had a good reason for beating her over the head, of course, but I thought maybe Marylou needed a moment before I launched into my explanation. She needed to own her anger, as she herself would have said if she hadn't been going bat-shit crazy and waving a gun at us.

"Do you even know how to use that?" Gerard asked calmly.

"Oh, I think I could figure it out," she said, spitting out a few tears as she spoke.

The tip of the rifle began to shake up and down a little.

"Marylou," I said, trying to keep myself under control, "put the gun down. Gerard isn't going to hurt us. He was *defending* us."

"You," she said, trying to bring her voice under control. "Sit. Both of you. Sit."

Gerard slowly lowered himself back into the chair where he'd been bound, and I sat near the television. Marylou kept the rifle high, pointed at Gerard. Large sweat marks had appeared under his arms and on his chest. We were all sweating. It was stupidly humid.

"The Law of Suspects," he said in a low voice. "My god. This is how eet happens."

"Shut up," Marylou said. "You *shot* him."

"And now you," Gerard said. "Eet's taken you. Do not hurt your sister. You must fight eet."

"I said shut up!"

She stepped right up to him and stuck the gun in his face. For the second time that night Gerard squarely faced death. This time he seemed calm. Maybe he was just getting used to it.

He stood, placing himself so that the barrel was pointed right at his heart.

"Shoot me," he said, "not your sister. Let eet end here. Shoot me. Shoot *me*, Marylou."

Gerard . . . this boy I'd only known for a few massively confusing hours, who'd tried to save me more than once . . . was now putting his life out for mine. Marylou had stopped shaking, and there were no more tears.

"Do eet," he said simply. "Because eef you don't, I'm going to take that gun from you."

"No," I yelled. "Gerard, don't. Marylou, don't!"

Marylou was trembling violently.

"I can do it to protect my sister and myself. . . ."

"I'm not going to hurt you."

"You son of a bitch! You killed—"

And then we both did something that will never completely make sense to me. I jumped from my chair and shoved Gerard out of the way. We fell to the floor together, me clocking my head on the edge of the table in the process. We landed on Henri's legs (and his blood and something squishy I'd prefer not to discuss). Marylou swung and reached for the trigger. I heard a click, click, click, and I was thinking, *This is the end. It ends with clicks. Click, click, click, like all the switches being turned off, all the lights going off on life.*

But the click, click, click was her trying to undo the safety, which Gerard must have put on. This delay gave Gerard enough time to get to his feet and punch my poor sister in the face. One blow, right to the jaw, and she went down for the second time in about fifteen minutes.

"Oh god," I said, rushing over to check her. "Oh god. God, she's going to be so *swollen*. . . ."

Gerard wasted no time. He took the ropes that had bound him before and tied her tight.

"Open the door," he said as he worked.

I backed up toward the front door, but he said, "*Non, non, non . . .* the cellar door. Here."

There was a thick, rough cellar door just on the other side of the stove. I had to jump over Henri's body and the running streams of blood to get to it. It had a plank of wood over it to bar it closed. I lifted this off.

"What are we doing?" I asked.

"Your sister is infected. The best thing we can do for her is make sure she is locked up until morning. Quickly, before she wakes."

There was no light switch, so I had to jump over Henri's body *again* to get the flashlight from the counter, where it had miraculously missed being splattered. And jump again to get back to the door. That was three jumps over his corpse. That seemed bad. So many aspects of this *seemed bad*, but it's amazing how quickly you can get used to a whole new set of circumstances.

The cellar was a raw old place, very small, with walls made of stones cemented together. It smelled like earth and was absolutely freezing cold. It looked like Henri mostly used it to develop film. There was a table of trays, shelves of chemicals, a clothesline of drying prints—most of them of trees and the mountains. There were also a few sacks of potatoes and onions, some bottles of wine, some homemade preserves on a different shelf, along with a few rounds of cheese in plastic containers. There were some shovels and garden implements in the corner. Henri's life had been so pleasant, so normal until recently.

"Let me find some blankets," I said. "And a coat."

"Be quick," he said.

I found an afghan on the sofa, a jacket in the hall, and took the rain slicker. I used them all to make a kind of nest for my unconscious, bound sister and helped Gerard carry her down the stairs. I tuck her in as carefully as I could as he lashed her to one of the supporting beams. I left the flashlight there, pointed up, to give her some light. Then we trudged back up the steps and shut the door, putting the beam across it.

"Is this really necessary?" I asked.

"Is what necessary?" Gerard asked. He had picked

the gun back up and was examining it.

"Locking her in the basement. Can't we just keep her up here?"

"Eet is better to keep her there. She is dangerous now. In the morning we will release her."

It made sense. Kind of. As much sense as anything could make. I looked down at poor Henri, his crumpled body on the floor.

"What do we do now?" I asked.

Gerard looked up at me and smiled.

Okay. So we made out on the couch for an hour. I don't think it's fair for anyone to be judging me. Yes, I know. Dead guy. Sister tied up in basement. I know, I know. But there was nothing else to do except watch *Mission: Impossible* in French. They say that stressful situations bring people together. It's true. No, it's really true. I'm sure there's something in the *DSM-IV* about it.

So yes. Couch, dark living room, rain outside, French countryside . . . the rest of the picture sounds right, doesn't it? We had just paused because our lips had gone a little numb when we heard Marylou screaming in the basement.

"She is awake," Gerard said calmly, stroking my hair.

I buried my head into his chest and put my hands

over my ears, but nothing drowned it out. She was screaming my name over and over.

"Can't we let her out?" I asked. "We have the gun. We can tie her up in the kitchen where it's warm. She's going to need water and food. . . ."

"She will be fine," he said. There was a firmness to his voice I didn't like.

"She can't hurt us," I said, sitting up. "There are two of us. I'm not saying that we let her run around, but . . ."

"You have no idea what she can do."

In the dark all I could see was the outline of his hair, his bright eyes. His hand was on my leg. I felt his fingers tighten and tense.

"The infection," he said, "you do not understand. You do not know what eet does. You have no idea. I have seen what eet does. That is not your sister right now, Charlie. She was gone by the time you got to the part about the guillotine."

"The part about what?"

"The part about the guillotine."

I went back through my mind, back to the moment where I was standing there with Henri and he was talking and talking and I asked to use his bathroom. . . . He had never said anything about a guillotine. I'd cut him off. I never got the whole story.

Which meant that possibly . . . possibly I had never been infected. I had never passed it on to Marylou.

But Gerard seemed to know a lot about this Law of Suspects thing.

And he was sounding calmer and calmer, the tone stripped from his voice, just like it had been from Henri's. But Gerard would never let himself listen to the story. . . .

Gerard had been tied up in a chair, alone with Henri. Helpless.

His fingers flexed again. He was staring at me in the dark, his expression unmoving.

"Right," I said, trying to sound cool. "That part. That was the *freakiest* part."

I couldn't take Gerard, not physically. All I had was the gun, and I was not going to shoot him. We hadn't known each other long, but I liked him. He was a good person. He had almost gotten himself killed trying to protect me.

"I was thinking," I said. "The car. We should really check the car. I'll bet there's enough gas. Henri was probably lying about that."

"Where is there to go?"

"To town!" I said.

"There is no point."

"I'd feel better if we just looked," I said. "I'll just go and check. It'll take two seconds."

I felt his hands moving to grab my arm, but I got up first.

"And I'll get us something to eat!" I said as cheerfully as I could. "Something besides onions!"

I hurried to the kitchen and fumbled around for the switch. We had turned the lights off because the sight was so horrible. I couldn't find the switch, so I made my way to the table in the dark and grabbed the gun. I had to move it. Hide it. Somehow get it out of the picture. But I got exactly nowhere, because Gerard was behind me in a moment.

"What are you doing?" he asked.

If there was ever a moment to lie, this was it.

"God," I said. "I tripped and *fell* on this. I tripped over his *leg*! God. This is so messed up!"

I staggered away, the gun still in my hands, but I continued making noises of general upset and confusion. It helped that Marylou was still screaming away.

"You should give me that," Gerard said quietly.

I stepped over Henri and put my back up against the cellar door, pointing the gun at him.

"I can't," I said. "Please, Gerard. Don't make me hurt you."

"Charlie? What are you . . ."

He sounded so confused, his little French accent peaking on my name. Like he was struggling with something inside himself.

"He told you the story," I said. "When you were in the chair. Didn't he? You couldn't help it. You couldn't get away."

"Eet gets only one person," he replied. "Eet has your sister."

"It doesn't have my sister. It has you. You know it. Please, Gerard."

He stepped closer.

"I have been hunting rabbits all my life," he said. "I can shoot very well. Give eet to me. I will protect both of us."

In the dark my fingers were feverishly trying to find the safety. I didn't even want them to. They looked for it on their own. Gerard stepped forward and put his hand over the barrel.

"Charlie," he said. "Eet is me. Eet is Gerard. Do not shoot me. Don't listen to eet."

"It hasn't got me, Gerard! I never heard the end of the story! Now back off. . . ."

And then my fingers found the safety. And I fired. And Gerard fell.

"Oh wait," I said to myself. "He did mention a guillotine. How did I forget that?"

❧

Here's the thing. . . .

God. It's hard to explain. I get so confused now. I start talking and I just forget what I'm saying halfway

uncan Branch Library
)3-746-1705

tle: Yoda Bird's heroes
all number: F ANG
em ID: 39012012383246
ate due: 9/28/2017,23:59
ate charged: 9/7/2017,18:17

tle: Vacations from hell
all number: 813.0108 VAC
em ID: 39012010715498
ate due: 9/28/2017,23:59
ate charged: 9/7/2017,18:17

itle: Plants vs. zombies.
imepocalypse
all number: F TOB
em ID: 39012012445649
ate due: 9/28/2017,23:59
ate charged: 9/7/2017,18:17

or your convenience,
ou can renew items online
t alexlibraryva.org.

through. I think it's all the meds I'm on. I pop pills all day long. They try all different combinations. Some work better than others. Today is one of the better days. I'm clear enough that they let me use the computer. The computer is usually way off-limits. I think they think I'm going to try to eat the keyboard or something.

They tell me it's been three months since I got here, since it all happened. It feels like two weeks or something, but I just looked out the window and all the leaves are off the trees. There's a splattered pumpkin at the end of the long drive, so I guess Halloween is either coming or it's already come and gone.

So I guess you want to know what happened?

As I remember it, I shot Gerard, and then a second or two later there was this massive cracking noise, like thunder, coming from inside my head. Everything went dark. According to the reports, if Gerard hadn't put his hand over the stupid barrel he probably would have been fine, but as it was I blew it off. I dropped the gun. He managed to keep himself together long enough to pick it up and club me with it with his remaining hand.

I woke up in the hospital. Marylou was there, holding my hand and telling me it would all be okay. Then I passed out again. I was unconscious a lot. Awake a bit in the hospital in France. Awake for a moment or two in the wheelchair at the airport. I do remember Gerard coming to see me before I left. His handless arm was in a sling. I was pretty out of it at the time, but he didn't look angry. I think he even stroked my hair.

The coroner determined that Henri actually did kill himself (powder on his hands or something). They found the rest of his wife's body exactly where Gerard said it was, along with ample evidence that Henri was the one who killed her. The dog was buried with her. This left the slightly more baffling problem of why one boy from the village and two American tourists ended up in a bloody confrontation in his house: one bound in the basement, another with no hand, a third unconscious on the kitchen floor. That this happened three days after a gruesome murder-suicide was even more troubling.

The final analysis was: Gerard was the hero, the one who noticed the disappearance of Henri's wife and kept watch over the house to see if anything suspicious was going on. When the two American tourists (us) came stumbling by, Gerard moved in to protect us. Flooded with guilt, Henri took his own life. And I, conveniently, lost my mind.

As to why this all happened at the same exact time, the local police had no idea—but several psychologists took a crack at figuring it out.

Based on my lying about Gerard attacking me, beating my sister over the head with a DVD player, shooting Gerard . . . it was determined that I had had a psychotic break. I wound up in a mental hospital just outside of

Boston. ("That's not what we like to call it," said Mary-lou. "It's a psychological rehabilitation facility.")

Now that I can access my e-mail, I see that Gerard sent me a message every single day. The first ones were really short, but as he got used to typing with the one hand he was able to say a lot more. He's the only person in the world who doesn't think I belong here. He can't wait until they let me out, which sounds like it won't be for a while. He says he's going to come and visit, just as soon as he's been fitted with the prosthetic hand.

And I just read Marylou's e-mail . . . the one with the link to her award-winning psych paper that she feels will secure her a place in one of the best grad programs. I read it. It detailed every aspect of the case.

Including the entire Law of Suspects story.

Including the part about the guillotine.

I'm logging off now and going back to my room. And I am going to ask them to up my meds. I like it here, nice and safe, with no sharp things and everyone all locked up. It is, as Gerard would say, better than the alternative.

The
Mirror House

CASSANDRA
CLARE

The two hours of washboard dirt road between the airport in Kingston and the tiny town of Black River would be bad enough even if I wasn't hung over from all that wedding champagne. As it is, I spend most of the time staring out the window and trying not to throw up. It isn't easy, especially since we keep passing dead animals on the side of the road and sometimes piles of burning garbage that stink like hot plastic.

My mom said Jamaica was going to be a paradise. But then again, this is the same woman who insisted that she and Phillip needed to leave for their honeymoon the morning after the wedding. Why they decided they had to bring me and Evan, Phillip's son, along with them on their trip, I'm not sure. They explained it to me—or at least my mom had, with Phillip sitting there glowering like he always did—as something about "family togetherness." But with Phillip dead silent as always and Evan scrunched up as far away from me as he can get on the van's sticky bench seat, I'm not sure how much togetherness we're really going to achieve. Of course, given what happened in the garden last night after the reception, togetherness is probably the last thing that Evan and I need.

The villa my mother has rented is much more beautiful than it looked in the online photos. The floors are shiny, dark as the polished outside of a walnut shell; the walls are blue, sponge-painted with a wash of green, calling up the colors of the sea and sky. One whole wall is missing, just open to the deck outside, the turquoise swimming pool and the cliff falling away to the white sand and dark sea beyond. The sun has just begun to set, casting widening rings of red, gold, and bronze over the water.

My mother stands in the arch of the doorway, her hand against her throat. "Oh, Phillip . . . look!"

But Phillip isn't looking. He's over by the front door with the pile of bags, speaking to Damon, the bellboy, in a low, gruff voice. Something about how Damon shouldn't be expecting a tip and anyway he could have carried his own damn luggage. Damon shrugs his white-shirted shoulders, philosophical, and leaves, stepping past Evan, who is leaning against the wall, staring down at his shoes. I can tell he's embarrassed by his father, but when I try to smile at him, his glance away from me looks like a flinch.

Phillip looks over at me. Maybe he sees the expression on my face—I'm not sure—but either way he still reads me all wrong. "Evan," he says, "take Violet's bags to her room."

Evan starts to protest. His father shoots him a look of disgust.

"Now, Evan."

Evan hoists the duffel over his shoulder and follows me to the room marked 3. It has louvered windows that look out over the deck, a skylight, and a huge white bed canopied with drifts of mosquito netting. Evan sets the bag on the floor with a bang and straightens up, his blue eyes flashing.

"Thanks," I say.

He shrugs. "Not a problem." I watch him as he glances around, watch the way the muscles in his shoulders move as he turns. "Nice room."

"I know." I laugh nervously. "The bed is huge."

The moment the words are out of my mouth, I freeze. I shouldn't have said that. I shouldn't even have said the word *bed* around Evan, not after what happened in the rose garden. He'll think I'm joking, being stupid, or he'll think I'm asking him—

"Guys! Dinnertime!" My mom pops her head

around the door, smiling brightly. I've never been so glad to see her.

"I'll be right there—I just need to wash my hands." I duck into the small bathroom while Evan skulks out on my mom's heels. The walls of the bathroom are tiled with ocean-washed glass in soft and dull blues, greens, and reds. I run the water in the bronze basin and splash some up on my face. When I glance into the mirror, I see that my cheeks are red as roses.

Dinner is served out on the deck, with our family sitting at a long, low table and the villa's staff bringing us bowls of food: heaping piles of potato salad, sharp vinegary slaw, fish cooked with garlic and Scotch bonnets, and a bowl of dark, fragrant curry full of lumps of simmering meat.

I try to turn as the bowls are passed to me to smile at the villa staff, but no one will meet my eyes. The staff is a blur of dark faces and hands, the gleam of a coral-and-gold bracelet as a hand retracts the salad bowl I'm done eating from. "Thanks," I say, but there is no response.

Phillip is forking up curry like it's going out of style. "What is this?" he says abruptly, spearing a chunk of meat on his fork and shoving it in his mouth.

The tallest of the cooks, a woman with a sharp-boned face and a white kerchief tied around her hair, says, "It is goat curry, sir."

Phillip spits the meat back onto his plate and grabs for a napkin, staring at the cook with accusing eyes.

I look down at the table, trying not to laugh.

The next day the heat is stunning, like a drug. I lie out on a lounger by the pool, the straps of my blue suit pushed down over my arms to avoid tan lines. My mom won't let me buy a bikini. Phillip is sitting over in the shade reading a book called *Empire of Blue Water*. Evan is sitting with his feet in the pool, staring into space.

I attempt to catch his eye, but he won't look at me, so I go back to my book. I try to read, but the words dance on the page like the sunlight dances over the pool water. This kind of weather makes everything dance.

Finally I put the book down and wander into the kitchen to get a Coke. The woman from last night, the tall cook who told Phillip he was eating goat, is standing by the sink washing up our dishes from breakfast. Today her headscarf is bright red, the color of a tropical bird.

She turns when she sees me. "What can I help you with, miss?" Her accent is as soft as flower petals.

"I just wanted a Coke." I get the feeling I shouldn't be in here, that the kitchen is the domain of the staff, even if all I want is a can of soda. Sure enough, instead of directing me toward the fridge, she retrieves the bottle herself, pops it open, and pours it into a glass for me.

"Thanks." I take it, the cool glass feeling good against

my fingers. "What's your name?"

"My name?" She raises her dark eyebrows. They're perfect arches, like she plucks them every day. "I am Damaris."

"Damaris and Damon," I say, and then wish I hadn't; I sound like a moron. Maybe she doesn't even know Damon well.

"He is my brother," she says, and glances out the window, a crease appearing between her brows. "*Your* brother has gone down to the beach, I see. You should tell him to stay away from the other houses along the road. Most of them are private, and not all of them are safe."

Not safe? I think. *As in guarded by vicious dogs or trigger-happy security guards?* But Damaris's lovely, blank face gives away nothing. I set the empty glass on the sideboard. "Evan is my stepbrother," I say as if it's important; somehow I want her to know. "Not my brother."

She says nothing.

"I'll tell him to be careful," I say.

The path that leads down to the water is sandy, fringed by rocks and scrubby grass. The beach arcs away to the south, lined with small, brightly painted houses in tropical colors: hot pink, acid green, frog-belly yellow. Ours is the last house, backed up against stone cliffs pocked with dark holes like raisins in a pale custard. I think the holes must be caves.

Evan is nowhere on the beach. In fact, no one is on the beach. It's a pale swatch of inviting sand that's somehow totally empty. I'm surprised not to see anyone out sunbathing, but as I follow the curve of the sand along the water, I see that most of the other houses are shut and bolted up. Some have heavy padlocks on their gates. They seem dusty, disused. The only one that looks like it might be inhabited is a hot-pink house, the color of a rose blossom, one of the closest houses to the villa. Its huge yard stretches down to the sand, surrounded by a wall covered in mosaic tiles that depict waves and sea creatures. The top of the wall is lined with bits of glass—not small jagged bits of glass meant to discourage intruders but big chunks of square and rectangular glass reflecting back the sea and sky. I glance through the gate and see a riotous garden of brightly colored flowers, but the door to the house is shut, the window curtains pulled across.

I'm surprised by the lack of activity. We can't be the only people staying in this area, can we? Travel brochures are always advertising "deserted beaches" as if it's something really desirable, but in reality it's kind of creepy. There are footsteps in the sand, so someone must have been walking here at some point, but there's no one visible.

I reach the end of the beach, turn and walk back

toward the villa. The sun beats down heavily on my neck and shoulders. It's cool up by the pool, but down here the heat feels like a heavy, wet blanket. I can see figures moving around up at the villa; they are black silhouettes outlined by the sun. As I near the path that leads back up through the scrub grass, a figure emerges from one of the holes in the rock.

It's Evan. He isn't wearing a shirt, just board shorts and flip-flops. His skin is as pale as mine is, but his wheat blond hair looks bright gold in the hot light. He has a few pale freckles splashed across his cheeks and nose, and I try to remember but can't if those are new or if he's always had them.

He looks surprised to see me. "Hey."

"Hey," I said, feeling, as I have since the wedding, stupid now that I'm around him. "Damaris told me to let you know that it isn't safe down here."

He squints, blue eyes against the sun. "Damaris?"

"The cook."

"Oh, right." He glances up and down the beach. "It looks safe to me. Maybe she meant there's a riptide or something."

I shrug. "Maybe." She didn't mean a riptide, but I don't feel like getting into it.

"Come on." He gestures at me to follow him. "I want to show you something."

He ducks back into the dark opening in the rock and

I follow, swallowing down my claustrophobia. I have to hold my breath to squeeze through a narrow passage, and then we come out in a larger space. Dim rays from outside spill through the opening slit in the stone, but they're not all that's providing illumination here: patches of glowing brightness are dotted here and there on the damp cave walls, and they're different colors too: ice blue and pale green and sheer rose. "Phosphorescent moss," Evan says. He runs his hand along the wall then shows the palm of it to me; it shines like the bright fin of a fish. "See?"

His eyes are glowing too, in the darkness. I remember the first time I ever saw Evan loping across the quad at school with his bag slung over his shoulder, his bright hair shining in the sunlight. He moved like someone with purpose, like there was a shimmering, invisible road only he could see and his feet were on it and he knew where he was going. I'd never seen him before—it turned out later he was new that year, having moved to town with his dad from Portland—and he didn't look like any boy I'd ever liked. I went for the hipster boys: worn jeans and glasses and serious hair. Evan was clean and sporty and he shone like gold in the sunlight, and from that moment I wanted him like I had never wanted anyone before.

Now I touch my fingers to his; they come away glowing, as if he's transferring his light to me. He tenses when we touch, and then his fingers wrap around mine. My toes dig into the sand as I go on tiptoe, reaching my face up to his, and then he's kissing me, and his mouth is damp and soft. His fingers dig tightly into my shoulders before he breaks away. "Vi," he says, and it's more of a groan than anything else. "We can't."

I know what he means. We went over all this before, the night in the garden, when we kissed and then fought for hours. *We have to tell them we can't tell them we can't do this they don't need to know of course they'll find out they'll kill us he'll kill me no. No.*

Evan moves past me toward the cave entrance and slithers out through it. I follow him, saying his name, squeezing through the narrow slit in the rock after him, and the strap of my bathing suit gets caught on a sharp piece of jutting rock, which is why it takes me a moment to untangle myself then join Evan on the beach. He's standing there, staring down the beach with his mouth open. When I follow his gaze, I see why.

There's a woman coming out of the pink house. She pushes open the blue-painted iron gate and walks out onto the sand. Except she doesn't just walk. She moves like a wave. Her hips roll, and her hair, which is long and white blond, ripples like foam on the sea. She's wearing a sort of printed sarong. It's split down one side, and you can see the whole of her perfectly tanned leg when she walks. She's got on a white bikini top, and the way she fills it out makes me want to cross my arms over my chest to hide how flat I am. She holds a bottle in one hand, the sort that my Coca-Cola came in earlier, though there's no label on it.

She pushes her glasses on her head as she comes close to us, and any hope I had that her face wouldn't match the rest of her vanishes. She's beautiful. Evan is just staring.

"You're the children from the villa," she says. She has a faint, indefinable accent. "Aren't you?"

Evan looks dismayed at being called a child. "I guess so."

She tilts the bottle in her hand. It's filled with a pale liquid that glows with an odd rainbow sheen in the sunlight. "It must be dull for you, being here in the off-season," she says. "Hardly anyone around. Except me. I'm here all the time." She smiles. "I'm Mrs. Palmer. Anne Palmer. Feel free to stop by my house if you need anything."

Evan doesn't look like he's about to speak so I do. "Thanks," I say stiffly, thinking that she doesn't look like an Anne. Anne is a plain, friendly name. "But we have everything we need."

Her lips curl up slightly at the corners, like burning paper. "No one has everything they need."

I reach to touch Evan on the shoulder. "We should get back to the house."

But he ignores me; he's looking at Mrs. Palmer. She's still smiling. "You know," she says, "you look like a nice, strong boy. I could use your help. I've got an old car—a classic, as they say—and it usually runs like a dream, but lately I've been having trouble starting it. Would you take a look at it for me?"

I wait for Evan to say that he doesn't know anything about cars. I've certainly never heard him mention them as a special interest. Instead he says, "Sure, I could do that."

Mrs. Palmer tilts her head back, and the sun glints off her hair. "Wonderful," she says. "I can't offer you much of a reward, but I've got a cold drink for you if you like." The bottle in her hand sparks rainbows.

"Great." Evan spares me only a single glance. "Tell the 'rents where I went, okay, Violet?"

I nod, but he doesn't even seem to notice; he's already heading toward the pink house with Mrs. Palmer. Evan never looks back at me, but *she* does; pausing at the gate, she glances back over her shoulder, her eyes skating over me in a thoughtful way that—despite the heat—sends a cold shiver racing up my spine.

Sunset comes and paints the sky over the ocean in broad stripes of coral and black. Damaris and the rest of the staff are setting the table on the porch. I sit at the edge of the pool, my feet in the water. I've been waiting for

Evan to come up the steps for hours now, but he hasn't appeared. Mom and Phillip are still sitting in their deck chairs, though Phillip has put down his book and they appear to be arguing in hushed, intense tones. I block them out, the way I always do when they fight, trying to concentrate on the sound of the sea instead. Everyone always says it sounds like the inside of a seashell, but I think it sounds like the beat of a heart, with its regular, pounding rhythm and the soft rush of water like the rush of blood through veins.

Holding a folded set of napkins in one hand, Damaris leans over the porch and says, "Will there be four of you for dinner or only three?"

"Four."

"I don't see your stepbrother here," Damaris says.

"He's down on the beach," I tell her. "But he'll come back."

Damaris says something under her breath. It sounds like, "They don't come back." Before I can ask her what she means, she turns back to setting the table.

Dinner is eaten in silence. No goat this time, just stuffed peppers and a lemony sort of fish. Halfway through the meal Evan joins us, sliding silently into his seat as if hoping not to be noticed.

Phillip freezes with his fork halfway to his mouth. "And where have *you* been?"

Evan stares at his plate. He isn't wearing his bathing suit anymore, I notice, but a fresh pair of shorts and a worn T-shirt. He looks very . . . clean. "I was helping the lady next door fix her car. She said if I could get it started, she'd let us take her boat out and use it if we wanted."

"That was very nice of you," says Mom. She turns to Phillip. "Wasn't it nice of him, darling?"

Phillip grunts a reply around his mouthful of fish. "I don't know why she thought you'd know anything about getting cars to work. You're just a kid."

Evan flushes but says nothing, concentrating instead on forking up food from his plate.

My mother turns back to Phillip. "So I was thinking, tomorrow maybe, we could take a trip to Black River."

"That town we drove through on our way here?" Phillip tears a chunk of bread in half. "It looked like a dump, Carol."

"Apparently there's a market there every weekend, with people bringing items from all around. And you can take boat trips up the river, see crocodiles in the water. . . ." My mother's voice trails off under Phillip's cold stare. "I thought it might be something for us to do as a family. Something fun."

"Fun?" Phillip echoes. "I didn't come all the way here, Carol, to shop for cheap handicrafts and stare at a floating log some idiot tour guide claims is a crocodile."

"But Phillip—" My mom reaches out for his hand and accidentally knocks over the glass bowl of fruit salad beside his plate. Phillip jumps up, swearing, even though none of it has gotten on him.

Mom looks dismayed. "I'm so sorry—"

Phillip doesn't answer her. He's staring coldly at the remains of the fruit salad on the tiles at his feet. "Look at this mess."

"Phillip." On the verge of tears my mom gets down on her knees, scrabbling with her fingers at the slippery bits of fruit and broken glass. I wonder where the staff is, but they seem to be hanging back, sensing the delicacy of the situation.

"Mom, *don't*," I say, but she ignores me. She has cut herself on the glass, the blood dripping down on the mess of squashed fruit and juice splashed across the ground. I look over at Evan, wondering if he'll say anything. He's always liked my mother, or at least I thought he did. But he stares silently at his plate and avoids my eyes.

That night I lie awake in my four-poster bed, staring at the ceiling. The mosquito netting, white as the veil of a bride, drifts in the faint breeze from the air conditioner. I can hear Phillip's voice on the other side of the wall rising and falling like a wave as it grows angrier and angrier. My mother's voice runs a faint point-counterpoint to his shouting: as his voice rises, hers gets more and more quiet. I watch a shining green beetle make its way across the stucco wall, its feelers reaching out delicately for something it can touch.

We don't go to Black River in the morning, of course. Phillip takes his book out to the pool and sits glowering in the shade. My mom stays inside, sunglasses over her eyes and a big hat casting dark shadows over her face, but despite the glasses I can still see that her eyes are swollen from crying.

Evan doesn't get up until noon, and when he does, he comes out of his room yawning, in board shorts and flip-flops. His hair looks lighter than before, as if the sun has already bleached out some of its color. I'm lying in the hammock on the deck, a magazine open on my lap; when I see him, I set it down and go over to him, lowering my voice as I get closer. "How did you sleep last night?" I ask, hoping he can read my eyes, wondering if he heard the same thing I did.

"Fine." He's not reading my eyes; his own sky blue ones are darting around nervously. Maybe he's wondering if they're watching us, if they're talking about how we stand too close to each other, talk too softly. But no. They don't notice anything. They never have.

I had met Phillip a bunch of times before my mother finally brought me over to his house, but that was the first time I'd ever realized how serious they were. Phillip was still trying to impress us both back then. He still thought there was some point in getting on my good side. He would come to our house dressed up in a suit, with a bunch of flowers for my mom and something for me—always something dumb and inappropriate, like a shiny barrette or a CD of bubblegum pop music. It was like he thought all teenage girls were the same and liked the same things, but he was *trying*, my mother said and besides he didn't know anything about girls—he only had a son. And even though I knew that, even though I knew Phillip had a son my age, I never gave him the slightest thought until that night, when my mom hurried me up the lighted walk to Phillip's front door and rang the bell, smiling nervously at me the whole time.

And Evan opened the door. He smiled when he saw me. "Hi," he said. "You must be Violet."

I stood there on the front steps without saying a word. I felt stunned, as if I'd fallen off a high tree branch and hit the ground hard, knocking all the wind out of me. There was just no way that this boy, who I watched every day at school, whose every mannerism I'd memorized—the way he flicked his hair out of his eyes or fiddled with his watch when he was bored—was the offspring of Phillip. Boring, tight-lipped, sallow-faced Phillip couldn't possibly have a son who looked like *that*.

I didn't even care that Evan didn't recognize me. Didn't care that he didn't seem to know we even went to the same school.

"Are you going down to the beach?" he asks now. "I'll come with you."

I shrug. There's really no way to stop him. "Okay."

There are baskets of beach towels on the deck, brightly striped as candy canes. Evan drapes one around his shoulders as we head down the sandy path to the beach. It's deserted again today, empty sand stretching away into the distance. It looks like an ad for some honeymoon destination, someplace where you can kiss on the beach with no one watching.

We spread our towels out and lie down, me on my stomach, Evan staring up at the sun. He has a book spread out over his stomach: *The Postman Always Rings Twice*, I think it is, though I can't read all of the spine. I was surprised when I found out Evan loves to read. I wouldn't have thought any boy who looked like he did had interests outside maybe sports and girls, just like I never would have thought he'd have any time at all for a skinny, unpopular girl who wore unmatching socks and boys' T-shirts because she didn't know what she was *supposed* to be wearing anyway.

But I found out I was wrong. Evan had time for me. The sort of time that meant we spent hours together in Phillip's library, talking or playing Halo on the big-screen TV. The sort of time that meant he actually waved to me in the hallway sometimes, even when other people could see him. The kind of time that meant that on Tuesday nights, when we had dinner at Phillip's, he'd wait for me outside school in his car, the parking brake on and the engine running, the passenger door propped slightly open. For me.

I'd slide into the seat, smile over at him. "Thanks for waiting."

He'd reach across me to pull the door shut. "No problem." The flush across the back of his neck as he bent to turn the key in the ignition let me know he noticed how close to him I was sitting.

Once we were so involved in conversation that even when we pulled up to Evan's house, we didn't get out of the car, just sat while it idled in the driveway, our voices mingling with the music from the car stereo. I reached to push a dangling bit of hair back behind my ear, but Evan's fingers were already there—hesitant, gentle against my skin. "Violet," he said when I went silent. "You know—"

The car's window shook as Phillip banged on it. "Evan."

Evan rolled the window down.

"Pull the car up into the garage" was all Phillip said, but one look at Evan's white face told me that the moment was gone forever.

"*Evan.*"

I think for a moment that it's my mother's voice speaking and half sit up, looking around for her. But the beach is still deserted. Evan is sitting up as well, and I follow his gaze to see Mrs. Palmer, the lady from the pink house, standing in her half-open gateway. She's too far away for me to have really heard her voice, and yet I could swear that I did, as if she were speaking in my ear. She is wearing a long pink dress today, almost the same color as her house, its halter neck leaving her brown shoulders bare. She has sunglasses on.

Evan is already standing, gathering up his towel. Sand glitters on his back and shoulders like a dusting of sugar. "See you later, Vi."

I crane my neck to look up at him. "But where are you going?"

"Anne said that since I helped her with her car, we could take her boat out on the water today." He seems to sense the way I'm looking at him, because he adds, "I'd bring you, but the boat holds only two people."

I say nothing, and he turns away—relieved, I think, that I'm not making a fuss. I watch him walk toward the house, the sun beating down like a hammer, and when he passes through the gate and Anne shuts it behind him, the sun seems to burst off all the shards of glass that decorate the front of it like an explosion. I shut my eyes against the hot, refracting light.

With nothing else to do, I wander up and down the beach, taking photos with the pink digital camera Phillip gave me as a present, back when he was making an effort to get me to like him. I had never particularly wanted a camera, but I amuse myself with it now, taking photos of bits of glass buffed by the ocean, the hulls of deserted fishing boats, the distant black line of the horizon. Words someone has written in the wet sand by the ocean's edge, already faded past readability. A sea horse washed up on the sand, its tiny mouth open and closing in drowning gasps. I throw it back out to sea.

On my way back to the villa, I stop and look out over the water. Anne's boat is there, drifting on the waves, its sail white as a dandelion clock against the dark blue sky. Though I can make out only the outline of a pair of shapes I think must be people, one thing is clear: Evan was lying. You could certainly fit more than two people on that boat.

My mother is silent at dinner, pushing her food around with her fork. Phillip ignores us both, humming to himself as he slices jerked pork onto his plate. It takes him a while even to notice that Evan isn't there, and when he asks where he is, I tell him that his son is in his room with a headache. I don't know why I'm covering for Evan. Maybe I just don't want to hear any more shouting.

Even hours after dinner the air still smells like jerk

spices. I lie in the hammock, looking at the stars. The air is heavy, heat-stunned, despite the darkness. The insects buzz wearily, clicking and fluttering their wings in the shadows. Somewhere in the distance I can hear the sound of music: loud, pulsing reggae. I look out to sea, wondering if I'll see a boat drifting on the sapphire water, but I see only a flat sheet of reflected moonlight.

"Some water, miss?" It is Damaris, her face a carved mask in the moonlight. She holds out a glass to me, iced with drops along the side.

I take it and hold it to the side of my head. "Thanks."

"Where is your stepbrother tonight?" she asks.

"Down on the beach somewhere."

"He is with that lady." Her eyes gleam in the moonlight. "The Palmer woman."

"I think so. Yeah." I flick a mosquito away from my knee; it leaves a bead of blood behind, like a tiny ruby.

"You should not let him see her. She is dangerous."

"Dangerous how?"

Damaris looks away. "She is not a good woman. She likes the strong ones and the pretty, young ones. She takes them and then they never come back. You should make him stay away from her, if you want to keep him."

Keep him? "And how am I supposed to do that?"

Damaris says nothing.

"I don't know why you're asking *me* to do something

about it anyway," I tell her.

She glances toward the villa. My mom and Phillip have already gone to bed; the lights are dark, except for the party light along the deck. "Because," she says, "no one else will."

In the morning when I wake up, Evan is asleep on the couch in the living room. He is shirtless still, twisted into an uncomfortable sort of position, with his arm under his head. There are marks like bruises beneath his eyes. He stirs when I come in and sits up slowly, blinking as if he doesn't recognize me. He hardly looks like someone who spent the day before relaxing out on the ocean.

"Evan?" I say. "Evan, are you all right?" I sit down next to him on the couch. I can feel heat radiating off him, off his bare skin, like a fever. "Did something happen yesterday?"

His eyes are like blue marbles. "I had a great time," he says, his voice as mechanical as a talking doll's. "It was a great day."

I watch from the railing of the deck as Evan goes down the path to the beach, takes a sharp right, and heads toward the mirror house. The gate swings open when he touches it, and he disappears inside. I look around. Phillip is gone, probably headed to the golf course, and my mother is reading a book in a lounge chair by the pool. I slide my feet into my flip-flops and head down the path.

The sand is hot, hot enough to burn my feet through the thin soles of my shoes. I limp until I reach the gate of the mirror house, and then, suddenly, the heat is gone and the sand is icy. The gate is closed, and through the bars I see the wild, growing garden with its riot of flowers, most of them planted in big old-fashioned stone urns. There are other things there too, now that I am looking closely: bits of what look like more mirrors, big shards of them set here and there in the sand as if Mrs. Palmer were hoping to grow a mirror tree out of the inhospitable ground.

I reach for the handle of the gate, only to realize there isn't one. There's a keyhole but no knob, and the bars of the gate are lined with bits of glass. They reflect my own face back to me, pale and anxious, as I peer through the bars hoping to see what's happening inside the house, but just as before all the curtains are drawn across the windows. I grab the bars and try to pull the gate open, but the jagged edges of the mirrors cut into my palms, and when I draw my hands back, they are bleeding.

The gate doesn't budge.

Back at the villa I head into the kitchen to wash my hands. I watch the pink threads of my blood mix with the water and swirl down the drain. When I turn away from the sink, I see Damon standing in the doorway watching me. He hands me a package of Band-Aids without a word.

Evan shows up for dinner this time but barely eats anything. The circles under his eyes look like they've been painted there. My mother tells him to be careful about getting too much sun.

Every night when I go into my bedroom, the comforter has been turned down, the sheets folded over it, the pillows fluffed. The windows are firmly shut, not letting in any of the humid night air; instead the air conditioner hums, cooling the room to near-freezing.

Lying on the bed, I wonder if Evan is in his room now, sliding under his covers, looking at the ceiling, thinking about me as I'm thinking about him. Or maybe he's wondering when the yelling will start up again. Or he could just be staring blankly into space like he was at dinner.

The tension started after the engagement. Phillip didn't smile as much. He was distant. I could feel his anger as if it were heat coming from an open oven. My mom fluttered around him like a butterfly, trying to please him, to make him smile again. I hated to watch. I couldn't tell if Evan did too. Not at first.

One night I was in the library with him playing Kingdom Hearts 2, mashing the buttons down hard like I was punching someone. Evan was beating me anyway.

Then the noise came up suddenly—the shouting, my mom's voice tearful and Phillip's angry—rising over the electronic beeps and yelps from the Xbox.

Evan dropped his controller with a thump and went to slam the door shut. When he turned to face me, he was breathing hard. "I hate him," he said. "I hate him."

I didn't say anything. I was thinking about how white he'd looked in the driveway that day Phillip had banged on the car window. How frightened. Except I wasn't sure if it was his face I was now picturing—his look of fear or my mother's.

"I didn't think anyone would ever marry him," said Evan. "I didn't think your mother would ever say yes. If I had . . ."

I should have made him finish that sentence, I think now, rolling over in the bed. As I reach to pull the pillow under my head, my hand strikes something: a lump, hard and cool like a piece of metal. My hand closes around it; I draw it out and stare. It is a key, made of dark metal with a twisted brass handle. It gleams dully in the moonlight.

I wake up still holding the key in my hand. I wash in the outdoor shower, wearing my bathing suit, watching the ocean roll while I rinse shampoo through my hair. I can see my mother and Phillip out by the pool. They are both reading, on side-by-side loungers, my mother in a cap with a colored plastic visor that turns her face bright blue. She is facing Phillip, her voice loud and animated, but his face is buried in his book and he isn't answering her. She might as well not be there at all.

The sand burns my feet through the flip-flops, but I have nothing else to wear. I endure the pain until the sand turns cold again outside Mrs. Palmer's house. It's almost noon, the sun directly overhead, and I feel it like a sharp nail piercing through layers of sky and into the skin at the back of my neck. Sweat trickles down into my bathing suit top as I work the key into the lock of the gate, twisting and jerking it until I hear the sound.

Click.

The gate swings open, and I step into the garden. I have to be careful, weaving my way through the shards of glass that stick out of the sand. A single one of them could slice off a toe if I stepped on it. I hardly look up at the house until I reach it; the rose pink is even brighter up close, the house made of a smooth, unremarkable stucco, a pattern of roses picked out along the side of it in bits of mosaic tile. There is a white rose painted on the front door, but I don't go up to it. I slide around the side of the house instead, feeling like a thief, an interloper. I see Mrs. Palmer's face again in my mind, her sunglasses like the eyes of a black fly, and I swallow against the dryness in my throat.

There is a window at the far side of the house that is open, just barely, a bit of curtain fluttering out into the still air like a banner. I raise myself on my toes, grab the ledge to get higher, and peer around the curtain into the room beyond.

It's a living room, with plain, hard, modern furniture, nothing like the luxurious tropical furnishings at the villa. A coffee table, a red couch, a bunch of flowers in a black vase, a TV whose screen is dusty as if it's rarely used. A square picture frame hangs over the couch, but it is backward, as if someone has turned the picture to the wall.

On the couch lies Evan. He seems to be asleep, his arm hanging limp down the side of the sofa, fingers brushing the floor. His hair has fallen over his face and moves slightly when he breathes, like seaweed in a current.

There is a rustle, and Mrs. Palmer comes into the room carrying a drink in her hand. There is ice in it and some slices of lime. It looks like a gin and tonic, one of Phillip's favorite drinks. She sets it on the table and turns to look at Evan. She's wearing a filmy sort of white cover-up over a black bikini and her sunglasses. Who wears sunglasses inside? And high heels? *Her feet must hurt*, I think as she bends over Evan. My stomach thuds dully as she brushes his hair back and leans in, her mouth over his, and I wait to see them kiss.

But she doesn't kiss him. She stays where she is, hovering, like a bee over a flower. Her blond hair falls behind them in a sheet of pale gold, and I think how I wish I had hair like that, and then I see her purse her lips as if she's about to start whistling. And Evan's mouth opens too, though his eyes are still closed. His chest is rising and falling fast now, as if he's running. I see his hand clench into a fist. Something pale white and faint as a wisp of smoke rises from his mouth; it looks like he's exhaling a puff of dandelion fluff.

Mrs. Palmer straightens, and reaches to flip over the hanging picture frame on the wall. It is a mirror, its surface strangely dull. She returns her gaze to Evan; the white smoke rising from his mouth has become a plume, and as it rises, the surface of the mirror begins softly to shimmer. She bends over Evan once again—

My hands lose their grip on the sill of the window and I fall, my ankle bending awkwardly under me, almost tipping me into the sand. My breath comes out in a whimpering gasp.

"Who is it?" I hear Mrs. Palmer call, her voice oddly thick. "Is someone there?"

I run.

* * *

My heart is pounding when I reach the villa, the soles of my feet burning. I duck into the kitchen through the back door, around the side of the villa where dusty flowers bloom in the shade. Damaris is not there; the kitchen is empty, plates and dishes stacked on a colorful kitchen cloth next to the sink. I turn on the water and rinse my dusty hands, my heart still pounding. *She is not a good woman. She likes the strong ones and the pretty, young ones. She takes them and then they never come back.*

I go out onto the deck; my mother is lying there in a lounger, half in and half out of the shade. She has a book open on her lap, the same one she's been reading all week. I don't think she's advanced more than a few pages into it. She looks up, sees me, and gestures for me to come over.

I sit down at the foot of the lounger, and my mom smiles at me faintly. "Are you having a good time, Violet?"

My mouth is dry; I want to tell my mother about what I've seen, about Evan, but she looks so distant, as if she's drifting away on a high sea. I try to remember the last time I felt like my mom was really concentrating on anything, especially me. "Sure."

"I feel like I've hardly seen you," she frets. "Still, I suppose it's better, you and Evan having fun together. . . ."

I think of Evan lying limp and gray-faced on the couch. "I'm worried about Evan, Mom."

"Worried?" Her gray eyes are vague behind her sunglasses. "You shouldn't worry while you're on vacation."

"No, I mean, I think there might be something wrong with him . . . like, really wrong."

She sighs. "Teenage boys can be sort of moody and cranky, Vi. Hormones coursing through them and all that. Just don't pay attention to his sulks. He has to get adjusted to this new family situation, just like you do."

"Mom," I say slowly, gathering up my courage. "Mom, are you happy?"

She sits up, looking surprised. "Of course I am! I mean, look where we are." She gestures widely, her arm taking in the sea, the sky, the beach. "Even with me working both jobs we could never have afforded this nice vacation before."

But it's not nice. It's on the tip of my tongue to say it, but the look on my mom's face stops me. It's like she's standing in front of me in a brand-new dress begging me to tell her she looks great and I can't bring myself to tell her the truth: that the dress is ugly, cheap-looking, stained, and tacky. Because I love her, I bite back the words.

She slips off her sunglasses and for a moment I think she's really looking at me, really seeing me. "I know

Phillip seems short-tempered," she tells me at last. "But he's just tired. His job is so demanding. Really, he loves us. I can see the kindness in him. In his eyes. You know?" She goes on without waiting for my response. "It's what's in someone's eyes that's important. Like the saying goes, eyes are the mirrors of the soul."

"Windows," I say.

She blinks. "What?"

"Eyes are the windows to the soul. Not mirrors."

She reaches forward and puts her hand over mine. It feels thin, her fingers hard and dry as twigs. "You're so smart," she says. "You know everything."

The front garden of the villa borders on a dusty unpaved road that stretches from here to Black River. A fence of bamboo blocks the house off from the occasional traffic, hiding us from the world. The garden itself is full of flowers: purple jacaranda, pink orchids, red bougainvillea. Damon is there, in the shade, a white hat tipped back on his head. He is inspecting one of the sprinklers. It all seems so normal that I feel foolish when I walk up to him and say, "I need to talk to your sister."

He looks at me, his dark eyes fathomless. "My sister?"

"Damaris," I say. "Please."

After a moment he flips open his cell phone, dials,

and speaks into it in such a hasty dialect that I can't understand any of what he's saying. After a moment he shuts the phone and turns to me with a curt nod. "She say wait for her under the flame tree." He gestures toward the big twisted tree with its red-brown blossoms. "Over there."

Standing under the tree, reddish blossoms shower down on me every time a breeze blows through the branches overhead. The faint brushes of petals against my neck and shoulders feel like the touch of insect wings on my skin. I have to fight the urge to gasp and flick them away. I am relieved when Damaris steps through the bamboo gate and walks over to me. She is wearing a cotton dress the colors of sunset, but her face is somber.

"You saw her," she says without preamble, "didn't you?"

It comes out in a rush: the gate, the key, the garden of broken glass, what I saw through the window. She watches me while I talk, her face immobile, until I am done, and I say, "Who is she, Damaris? What is she?"

"You really want to know?" she asks.

"I do," I say. "Please tell me."

"She is a witch," says Damaris. "A very old one. Not all magic is bad, but her kind is. She owned a plantation once, or at least her husband did. They say he used to beat her. One day she rise up, kill him with her own hands. Then she start to kill the slaves, one by one. Just the men, you understand. She make them love her, and then she suck the life from them and leave them to die as husks, like empty seed-pods. She like the young and the pretty ones, but if she cannot take those, she will take any man. She lure them with a magic drink, and once they have a taste, they are hers. She take their souls and feed on them so she can stay young and beautiful. For hundreds of years she has done this. Sometimes she kill them quick, sometimes she wait, play with them for a while. Like she playing with your brother."

"Evan is not my brother," I say through my teeth. "And if you know all this, if everyone knows, then why don't you do something about it?"

"She cannot die," says Damaris. "Long ago they killed this woman and buried her in a grave with special markings to keep her from walking again. But even that will not hold her in the earth. Her magic is strong and deadly and she lives forever. Harm her and she will have her vengeance on you and your children after you. But you—you are a foreigner. You are leaving, going where she can't hurt you. So I can tell you how to hurt her. She feeds on the souls she takes. Destroy those, and you will take her power long enough to get your stepbrother back."

"But where does she keep them?"

"I do not know where they are," Damaris says. "But you are a clever girl. Maybe you can figure it out." She eyes me sideways. "I tell you one thing, though. Anne Palmer never give up a man once she have her claws in him. Not for nothing."

"Then why are you telling me all this?" My voice rises almost to a scream. "If there's nothing that can be done to save Evan, if it's too late, then what's the point?"

A red flower detaches itself from the tree overhead and drifts down to rest on Damaris's shoulder like a splash of blood. "I say she never give up a man for nothing," she says. "I never say she wouldn't do it for something."

That night Evan isn't at dinner. Phillip frowns at his son's empty place, a sharp line appearing between his eyebrows as if sliced there with a knife. "Violet," he says—he always draws my name out when he speaks it, as if preparing to lecture me: *Vi-oh-let.* "Violet, where is Evan?"

I look at my plate. There is curry piled on it, and fish wrapped in banana leaves, and jewel-toned sliced fruit. The sight turns my stomach. "At the beach, I think."

"Well, go get him." He picks up his fork. "I've had enough of him missing family meals."

I glance toward my mother, who nods imperceptibly,

as if afraid to be seen giving me permission. I throw my napkin down and stand up. "I'll see if I can find him," I say. *No promises.*

The sun has gone down, leaving the sand cool and soft under my feet. There is a breeze off the ocean; it blows through my hair, cooling the damp sweat on the back of my neck, between my shoulder blades. I turn to look at Mrs. Palmer's house. It is dark and lightless under the dimming sky, like a flower whose petals have closed for the night. I think of what Damaris said to me, and then I think of Mrs. Palmer's terrifying face as she bent over Evan, and my heart twists inside me. I can't go in there. I can't help or save him. I don't know why Damaris even told me anything. She's seen my mother and Phillip together. It ought to be obvious that I'm not someone who can save anyone, even people I love.

I turn back toward the villa, and that's when I see it: a scrap of blue caught on one of the rocks by the cave entrance Evan showed me the first day we were here. A blue the same color as Evan's shirt. I move toward the cave, check to see if anyone's watching me, then turn sideways to slip inside.

I push through the narrow part of the short tunnel, and then I've come out in the larger space where the colored moss glows against the cave walls like party lights. It takes me a moment before I see Evan, sitting on the damp sand at the base of the cave wall, his legs drawn up, his face in his hands.

"Evan." I kneel next to him. "Evan, what's wrong?"

He looks up, and I'm shocked. Even in the short amount of time between yesterday and this evening, his face seems to have fallen in on itself: he is sunken and gray, his eyes outlined by stark shadows. His shoulders look thin beneath the worn blue material of his T-shirt. Before, he seemed mechanical, deadened, like someone on a numbing drug. Now the drug has worn off and he's shaking and desperate. It's much worse somehow.

"Vi," he whispers. "Something happened—I made her angry. I don't even know what I did, but she told me to go away."

"Mrs. Palmer? Is that who you mean?" I reach to touch him, slide my hand over his shoulder, squeeze hard. He barely seems to notice. "Evan, you shouldn't be around her. She's not a good person. She's not . . . good for you."

"I *have* to be around her," he said. "When I'm not around her, I feel like I can't breathe. Like I'm dying." He picks fretfully at the sand. "You wouldn't understand."

Oh. That hurts. Like I'm just a little kid who can't feel anything. I suck in my breath. "Do you love her?"

He gives a dry sort of cackle, not really a laugh at all. "Do you love water? Or food? Or do you just have to have it?" He leans his head back against the cave wall. "I think I'm dying, Violet."

"We'll get you home," I say. "We'll go home, and you'll forget all about her."

"I don't want to forget," he whispers. "When I'm with her, I see . . . everything. I see *colors*. . . ."

"Evan." My cheeks are wet with tears; I reach to touch his chin, to turn his face toward me. "Let me help you."

"Help me?" he says, but it sounds more like, *please help me,* and he opens his eyes. I lean toward him, and our lips meet somewhere in the middle of all this darkness, and I remember kissing him at the wedding reception, when we were both a little drunk and giggling under the canopy of fake white flowers in the garden. That kiss tasted like champagne and lipstick, but now Evan tastes like sea and salt. His skin feels dry under my hands as I slide them over him. Even as he rolls on top of me and I hold him in my arms, he feels as light as driftwood, and when he cries out a name, the name is not my own.

I practically have to push Evan back up the path to the villa. When we get there, I see that my mother and Phillip are done eating: the table is abandoned, flies gathering thickly around a plate of fried plantains. I push Evan down on a lounger, where he sits limply, his head in his hands.

"I'll be right back," I tell him, though he barely seems to hear me.

I head inside through the double doors. I'm not sure what I'm thinking now—that if I beg my mother and Phillip, they'll take us home on the next plane, cutting our vacation short? That they'll take Evan to the hospital, anything to get him away, even if Damaris says it won't make any difference?

Their bedroom door is shut; I stop in front of it, my hand up, about to knock. There are voices audible from the other side: Phillip shouting, my mother saying something, trying to calm him down, but it isn't working. His voice rises even as hers spirals down into soft gasps. She's crying. My hand is frozen in midmotion like a statue's. My mother's sobs roll softly under the door like the sound of the tide being sucked back out to sea, cut off suddenly by the sound of a slap, sudden as a gunshot. I hear her gasp, and suddenly everything is quiet.

"Carol . . ." Phillip says. I can't tell if he sounds sorry or just tired. I am not sure I care. *It will always be like this*, I think, *for the rest of my life, listening through a closed door as Phillip slowly destroys my mother, bleeding her soul dry as surely as Mrs. Palmer is bleeding Evan's.*

I step away from the door and the silence on the other side of it. In the living room Phillip's golf clubs gleam in the leather bag that hangs from one of the hooks beside the front door. I grab a nine-iron and walk out onto the deck. Evan is lying on the lounger where I left him, his head on his crooked arm. He is so still I have to check the faint rise and fall of his chest to see that he's still alive before I turn toward the path that leads down to the ocean.

The sea at night is black as ink. If I were a ghost flying over it, I wonder, could I see my face in its mirrored surface? It pounds onto the beach, sending up white froths of spray, as I slip through the gate of Mrs. Palmer's house and into the garden.

Everywhere the shards of glass slice up out of the sand like shark fins slicing through water. The air here by the ocean is thick and hot to breathe. I raise the nine-iron in my hand; it feels heavy and solid. I bring it down hard against the nearest shard, half expecting the club to bounce off it. But the glass shatters, spiderwebbing out into a million cracks. A white puff of smoke rises from it, like an exhalation of cigarette smoke, and dissipates into the night air.

I stand there breathing hard, holding the club. And then I swing again, and again. The air is full of the lovely, silvery sound of shattering glass. A light goes on suddenly—the porch light of the house—stabbing into my eyes, but I keep swinging, bashing glass after glass after glass, until something seizes the other end of the nine-iron and it's wrenched viciously out of my hand.

Mrs. Palmer is standing in front of me. She no longer looks perfectly put-together; her hair is damp and tangled, her eyes wide and wild. She's wearing a long black dress, cap-sleeved, old-fashioned. She really does look like a witch. "What do you think you're doing?" she half screams. "This is private property, *my* property—"

"These don't belong to you," I tell her. My voice is steady, but I can't help backing up a step or two; my flip-flops crunch on the ground. "They're souls."

She gapes at me. "Souls?"

"Whatever you want to call them. The lives you've stolen. You put them in the mirrors. That's where you keep them."

Her voice is a snarl. "You're crazy."

"I saw you do it," I tell her. "I saw what you did to Evan. I was looking through the window."

Her mouth opens, and then I see her eyes go to the key in my left hand. "*Damaris*," she says. "That woman is a meddler. She never knows when to stay out of other people's business."

"I want you to leave my stepbrother alone," I tell her. "I want you to let Evan go."

Despite her anger her red lips curl into a smile. "Damaris must have told you it's not that easy."

"If you don't let him go, I'll come back—I'll smash

the rest of these—I'll tell everyone where you're keeping the souls, and then everyone will know—"

"Your stepbrother," she says. "He used to talk about you. He knew you had a crush on him. He said he found it amusing." The anger is gone from her voice now; it has a lilt to it, the way she'd talked to Evan when she offered him the bottle of juice. "You were a joke to him, Violet. So why are you putting so much of your energy into saving him now?"

It hurts, what she says. I tell myself she's lying, but it hurts anyway, a sharp sting, like getting lemon juice in a shallow cut. I take a breath. "I love him. Damaris said he could only be helped by someone who loves him—"

"But he doesn't love you," she says. "That is how men are. They take the love you give them and they twist it until it becomes a stick to beat you with." She glances at the club in her hand; her look is vicious. "Tell me I have no right to even the score, Violet. Tell me you wouldn't do the same in my place. Men are a curse on women's lives and you know it."

In my mind I see Phillip and my mother at his feet, picking fruit off the ground with bleeding fingers. "I don't know what I think about men," I say. "But Evan is only a boy. He isn't good or evil or anything else yet. He shouldn't be punished."

"He will grow up to be like the rest of them," says

Mrs. Palmer, who murdered her husband in his own bed. In a distant sort of voice, she continues, "They all do. That is why I will not give him up."

I think of Anne Palmer's husband, the man with the stick. "Damaris said you wouldn't give Evan up for nothing," I say. "But he's young and weak. What if I could find you something even better?"

Against the darkness, like the sudden, startling gleam of a firefly's light, I see Anne Palmer's smile. "Tell me," she says.

I wake in the morning to bright sunlight and the sound of birds. I lie in my netted bed for a long series of moments. It would be easy to think that last night never happened, any of it, but when I turn my head, I see the plastic bottle sitting on my bedside table next to the alarm clock. The pale liquid inside it shines with a rainbow slipperiness, like an oil slick.

I throw on a batik beach dress and slide my feet back into my flip-flops. There are cuts speckled across my ankles where flying glass sliced my skin, but I am fairly sure that no one will think the red dots are anything but mosquito bites. I pick up the bottle on my way out. It feels heavy, heavier than if it were full of water. When I tilt it, the liquid inside makes a thick, sloshing sound.

Damaris is in the kitchen, frying bacon in a pan. She

says nothing, but I can see her watching me out of the corner of her eye as I take a highball glass from the cupboard and fill it with ice. I unscrew the top of the plastic bottle Mrs. Palmer gave me last night and pour the liquid over the ice. It glops slowly out of the bottle neck, thick as lava. It smells vaguely medicinal, like herbs. As I stare at it, Damaris reaches around me and drops a slice of lemon into the glass. "There," she says. "Tell him it is for his headache."

I nod at her and take the glass out onto the deck. Evan is still lying in his lounger, but now his eyes are open and there is some color in his skin.

He won't remember anything? I said to Mrs. Palmer last night in her glass garden, souls like bits of shining jagged teeth glittering all around us. *You promise?*

He won't remember, she had promised. *Only the vacation. The sun. The sand. And then the accident.*

My mother is sitting in a chair next to Evan, fussing and trying to get him to hold a cold washcloth against his face; he pushes her hand away fretfully, but at least his voice is strong when he tells her no. She is wearing dark sunglasses again, but they don't hide the discolored skin of her cheek. I take a long look at both of them before I cross the deck to the shaded alcove where Phillip sits with the newspaper open on his lap.

"Hi," I say.

He looks up, his narrow, cold face expressionless in the sunlight. There is no guilt in the way he looks at me, no inner admission that last night he did something that, even if my mother forgives, I do not. But I doubt Phillip is interested in my feelings, either way. He has never thought of me as a person at all, with the power to bestow forgiveness or withhold it.

It has to be fast, not slow, I'd said to Mrs. Palmer. *I don't want it drawn out. I want you to take it all at once.*

She'd smiled with sharp, white teeth. *All at once*, she'd promised, and handed me something flat and shining and sharp. A bit of broken mirror.

Evan's soul.

It's yours, she said. *To keep, or to break it open to return it to him entirely.*

I slid it under my bed last night, where it lay reflecting the moonlight. *I'll break it open tonight*, I told myself. *Break it and give Evan back his soul.* I'll do it tonight.

Or tomorrow.

I thrust the drink out toward Phillip. In the sunlight it looks like ordinary water, with a pale lemon wedge floating in it. Still, I can hear the hissing whisper of the thick liquid sliding over the ice. Or maybe I'm imagining that. "Here," I say. "Damaris sent this out for you. She said it would be good for your headache."

He frowns. "How did she know I had a headache?" I

say nothing, and after a moment he sets the newspaper down and takes the glass from my hand. "Thank you, Violet," he says in that stiff, formal way of his.

And he takes a swallow. I watch his throat as the liquid goes down. I have never watched Phillip with such fascination before. At last he sets the glass down and says, "What kind of juice is that?"

"Aloe," I tell him. "Damaris says it's good for healing."

"Folk nonsense." He snorts and reaches for his paper again.

"There's one more thing," I say. "That woman, the one Evan was helping, well, her car's still broken. She said Evan couldn't figure out how to fix it."

Phillip snorts. "I could have told her that. Evan doesn't know anything about cars."

"She was hoping you'd take a look at it for her," I tell him. "Since you know. You probably know more about this stuff than Evan does."

"That's right. I do." He picks up the glass again, drains it, and smacks his lips. "I guess I ought to go help the poor woman out." He stands.

"That would be great." I point down the path. "She lives there, in the pink house, the one that looks like a flower. She's expecting you."

And she is. *He's my stepfather*, I had told Mrs. Palmer. *He's strong, stronger than Evan. Older. And he hits my mother. Just like your husband hit you.*

Phillip pats my shoulder awkwardly. "You're a good girl, Violet."

No, I think. *That is one thing I am not.* Because somewhere in the pink house, Anne Palmer is waiting, Anne Palmer with her red lips and her garden of glass, and her mirrors that take your soul. I watch as Phillip jogs down the path, a little stiff in his new flip-flops, the sunlight bouncing off his head where he's starting to go bald. I watch, and I say nothing. I watch, because I know he is never coming back.

Nowhere
Is Safe

LIBBA BRAY

ello? We recording? I see a red light, so I'm hoping my battery lasts. Okay, pay attention, because I've got only one shot at this, and it's gonna come at you on the fly. If you found this on YouTube, you are seriously lucky, because you need to know this.

Sorry about that banging in the background. It's too hard to explain right now, and you don't want to know what's on the other side of that door. Trust me.

My name's Poe, by the way. Poe Yamamoto. And that's Poe as in Edgar Allan. Yeah, 'cause what guy doesn't want to be saddled with that name? Crap, I'm all over the place. Okay. Focus, dude. Tell the story.

Let's say you've just graduated high school and you've decided to celebrate the end of thirteen years of compulsory education with a little backpacking trip in

Europe with some friends. You do the do: Paris, Dublin, Venice—which, by the way, smells like pigeon shit fried in grease—London (cold, wet, expensive, but you knew that), maybe some beers in Germany. And just maybe one of you says, "Hey, let's go off the grid, check out some of these mysterious towns in Eastern Europe, hunt for vampires and werewolves and things that go bump in the Slavic night." Why the hell not, right? You're only doing this once.

So you pack it up and head east. You take a train through the kind of forest that's older than anything we have here, older than anything you can imagine. Like you can practically smell the old coming off that huge wall of forever trees, and it makes you feel completely small and untested.

Anyway.

You get to a village and you notice the big honkin' evil-eye pendants the locals hang from their windows. Maybe you even laugh at their quaint superstitions. That, my friend, is the kind of arrogant crap that can get a guy killed. It's not quaint and it's not superstitious. There's a reason those villagers are still alive.

You hang out, eat thick, spicy stew, try to make conversation with the locals, who keep telling you to move on—go see Moscow or Budapest or Prague. Like they want to get rid of you. Like you're trouble. You ignore them, and one day you and your friends might find yourselves venturing into that unfamiliar forest, winding through a thick mist that comes up out of nowhere. This is not the time to stop and take a piss on a tree or make a travelogue video for your family back home.

You know that prickly feeling you get on the back of your neck? The one that makes you scared to turn around? Pay attention to that, Holmes. That is a Me-No-Likee signal creeping up from the lizard part of your brain—some primal DEFCON center of your gray matter left over from the very first ancestors that hasn't been destroyed by gated communities, all-night convenience stores lighting up the highways, and a half dozen fake Ghost Chaser shows on late-night cable. I'm just saying that lizard part exists for a reason. I know that now.

So if you're walking down that unfamiliar path and the mist rises up out of nowhere and slips its hands over your body, turning you around until you don't know where you are anymore, and the trees seem to be whispering to you? Or you think you see something in the dark that shouldn't exist, that you tell yourself can't possibly exist except in creepy campfire stories? Listen to the lizard, Holmes, and do yourself a favor.

Run. Run like Hell's after you.

Because it just might be.

We still recording? Good. Let me tell you what happened, while I still can.

I don't know who got the idea first—might have been me. Might've been Baz or Baz's cousin, John. Could even have been my BFF, Isabel. Just three guys and a girl with backpacks, Eurorail passes, and two full months before we had to report to college. Somehow we'd managed to blow through most of our money in a month. That's when one of us—again, I can't remember who—suggested we stretch our cash by packing it through Eastern Europe.

"It's that or we go home early and spend the summer at the Taco Temple handing bags of grease bombs through the drive-thru window," Baz said. He was on his fourth German beer and looked like a six-foot-four, sleep-deprived goat the way he staggered around. There was foam in his new chin scruff.

"Can't we go to Amsterdam instead? I hear you can smoke pot right out in the open," John pleaded.

Isabel shook her head. "Too expensive."

"For you guys," John mumbled.

"Don't be that way," Isabel gave him a kiss, and John softened. They'd been a thing since the second week in Europe, and I was trying to be cool with it. Izzie was worth ten of John, to be honest. "So where should we go? Not someplace everybody and their freaking aunt Fanny go. Let's have a real adventure, you know?"

"Such as, my fine, travel-audacious princess?" said Baz, being all Bazlike, which is to say just one toe over the friend side of the Cheeky-Friend-or-Obnoxious-Jerk divide. He tried to pat Isabel's faux hawk. She shook him off with a good-natured glare and a threatened punch that had Baz on his knees in mock terror. "Mercy," he cried in a high voice. Then he winked. "Or not. I like it either way."

With a roll of her eyes Isabel opened our *Europe on the Cheap* travel guidebook and pointed to a section entitled "Haunted Europe" that gave bulleted info about off-the-beaten-path places that were supposedly cursed in some way: castles built out of human bones, villages that once hunted and burned witches, ancient burial grounds, and caves where vampires lurked. Werewolf or succubus hot spots—that sort of thing.

John tickled Isabel and grabbed the book away. "How about this one?" He read aloud, " 'Necuratul. Town of the Damned. In the Middle Ages Necuratul suffered from a series of misfortunes: a terrible drought, persecution from brutal enemies, and the Black Death. And then suddenly, in the fifteenth century, their troubles stopped. Necuratul prospered. It escaped all disease and repelled enemy attacks with ease. It was rumored that the people of Necuratul had made a pact with the devil in exchange for their good fortune and survival.

" 'Over the past century Necuratul's fortunes have dwindled. Isolated by dense forest and forgotten by industrialization, most of its young people leave for the excitement of the cities and universities as soon as they can. But they return for the village's festival day, August 13, in which Necuratul honors its past through various rituals, culminating in a Mardi Gras–like party complete with delicious food and strong drink. (Necu-ratul is famed for its excellent wines as well as its sup-posed disreputable history.)

"'Sadly, this may be the last year for the festival—and Necuratul itself—as there are plans to relocate the town and build a power plant in its location.'"

"Wow. There's a happy travelogue," Baz cracked. "Come to our town! Drink our wine! Ogle our women! Feast on our feast days! And all it will cost you is . . . *your soul!*"

"They've got great wine and a hellacious party? I'm there," John said. He still had his expensive sunglasses perched on his head. His nose was sunburned.

Baz drained his stein and wiped his mouth on his arm. "I'm in."

"Me too. Poe?" Isabel held out her hand to me and grinned. It was always hard to resist Izzie when she was being adventurous. We'd been best friends since seventh grade when she'd immigrated from Haiti and I'd arrived from the big city, and we'd held on to each other like buoys lost on a dark, uncertain sea. I laced my fingers through hers.

"Town of the Damned it is," I said, and we all shook on it.

The next morning we left the hostel before dawn and caught a train headed east from Munich. The train chugged around mountains with steep drop-offs that

made the still-hungover John and Baz sick to their stom-
achs. After a few more twists and turns we disappeared
into a deep, dark forest—a towering guard of ancient
power.

"I wouldn't last a day in there," I muttered.

"Dude, no one would," John said. He pulled his hat
over his face to block the light and went to sleep against
Isabel's shoulder.

At Budapest there was an influx of travelers, and our
cozy cabin was invaded by an old lady with a smell like
garlic and an accent dense as brown bread. "I am sitting
here, yes? You will make room."

Isabel and John were still asleep on the bench oppo-
site us, so Baz and I scooted over, and the old lady sat
down and spread out next to us. "Where are you going?
No, wait! Don't tell me. I guess. You're going to—"

"Necuratul. Town of the Damned," Baz interrupted.
He wiggled his eyebrows for effect.

The lady grunted. "I said I would guess. I am a
fortune-teller. When stupid American boys don't beat
me to the fist."

"You mean 'to the punch'?" Baz asked.

"Whatever. You are?"

We introduced ourselves and she nodded like she had
mulled it over and decided it was okay for us to have our
particular names. "You may call me Mrs. Smith."

Somehow Mrs. Smith didn't seem like the name of an
Eastern European fortune-teller who smelled of garlic

and got on at Budapest. I guess our faces gave it away, because she gave us a little shrug. "It was easy to paint on my truck. Besides, everybody knows someone named Smith. Come. I will tell your fortunes."

"We don't have any money," I said quickly.

"Who said anything about money?" Mrs. Smith snapped. "I forgot my book and I'm bored. Don't be such an asshole."

"Isn't this what happens in the movies a lot? There's some old dude or woman who tells your fortune and is all, 'Oh, you're gonna die or make a boatload of money or meet a girl. Now give me all your cash'?" Baz yammered.

Mrs. Smith bristled. "I can tell your fortune right now without even consulting your palm."

"You can?"

"Yes. You are an idiot. You will always be an idiot."

Baz's smirk disappeared. "'kay. In the movies it's usually more complicated. And less abusive."

Mrs. Smith was staring at my face, and I automatically felt my armor coming on. Like it was the first day of seventh grade all over again: *Yo, slant eyes. Gook. Sushi roll. Hey, you're Asian—can you help me with my math homework?*

"Something wrong?" I said with a lot of edge.

"You have one blue eye and one brown," she said.

I folded my arms over my chest like I was daring her to get into it. "Yeah. Genetic fluke. My dad's Japanese.

My mom's American."

"And totally hot," Baz interrupted. "I mean your mom, not your dad. I mean your dad's a good-looking dude and all, but your mom—"

"Baz. Stop."

"'kay."

"There is a legend about the man with eyes that see the earth and the sky. One brown, one blue," Mrs. Smith said. Her voice had changed, gotten softer, a little wary.

"What legend is that?"

"He is cursed to walk in two worlds, the living and the dead. May I?" She took my hand and stared at it a long time, frowning. "It is as I thought. You move hand-in-hand with the unseen forces, the dark spirits, the unquiet and vengeful. It is your fate to bump asses with evil, Poe Yamamoto, and very soon you will be tested."

"Dude," Baz whispered in my ear, his white-boy dreads tickling the side of my face. "Did the creepy old lady just say 'bump asses with evil'?"

She slapped his arm. "I am not deaf, you know."

"Ow! Was that necessary?"

"You were being fresh," Mrs. Smith said emphatically.

Baz shut up then. Anybody who could shut Baz up was a force to be reckoned with, as far as I was concerned.

"Beware the easy answer, Poe Yamamoto. Look beyond the surface to what lies underneath. There is always more. Another explanation. A deeper, more frightening truth. But without truth there is no resolution. And without that the dead do not rest."

"Okaaaay. Anything else I should know?" I asked.

"Yes. Don't eat the pastry in the café car. That's not fortune-telling. That's experience—it's always three days past stale and hard as brick." She handed me her card. It read: MRS. SMITH. FORTUNE-TELLER. There was a phone number in raised print. "In case."

"In case what?"

"You make it back." She gathered her things and shoved them into her handbag. "Okay. Now I move to another cabin. To be honest, you give me the willies. Good luck, Poe Yamamoto."

The door closed with a bang behind Mrs. Smith. Isabel woke up and stretched. She looked pretty all sleepy, the sunlight dappled across her ebony cheekbones. "What did I miss?"

"Forest. Mountains. More forest. Oh, and some bizarro fortune-teller lady just told Poe he's got a destiny with evil."

Isabel blew into her hand, made a face. "Yeah, well, I think it may be my breath. I'm going to the café car for gum."

It was well after dinnertime the next day when we reached the station closest to Necuratul, and everyone was suffering from tight muscles and hungry bellies. We showed the station agent our guidebook, and he pointed us toward a driver in a festive hat with a feather stuck into the band. He was sitting beside a horse-drawn wagon and eating a sandwich. Isabel pointed to the word *Necuratul* in the book, and the guy stopped chewing and gave us all funny looks.

"You should go to Bucharest or Prague. Very beautiful," he said.

"We really want to see the festival," Isabel said. She smiled her I-will-make-you-like-me smile, but it didn't work on this guy. He didn't crack so much as a grimace.

The driver picked at his sandwich. "They say they used to worship the devil. Some say they still do."

Baz made a vampire face, hooking his teeth over his bottom lip and opening his eyes wide. Isabel slapped his arm.

"Next year," the man continued, "they will build a power plant on the mountain. Good-bye, Necuratul. That is progress, they say. Anyhow. You have money?"

"A lot of money," Baz said at the same time John said, "Not much."

"Young people," the driver grumbled as he wiped his hands. "I will take you. But first I will tell you: do not go into the forest. Stay inside the stones and do not cross them or you will be sorry."

"Why will we be sorry?" Isabel asked.

"Restless spirits, waiting to be set free. Stay out of the forest," he warned, and offered the rest of his sandwich to his horse.

"That was a nice touch of creepitude," John said as we climbed into the back. "You think they pay him extra to add that little bit, like when you take the Jack the Ripper walking tour in London and they keep warning you about how he was never found and then some cheesy actor in a black cloak walks past really fast?"

"Maybe," I said, but the driver didn't seem like he was playing around. That's when I noticed the low stone wall bordering the forest on either side of the skinny dirt road. Streaks of white powder ran alongside it. Behind us I couldn't even see the train station anymore, only thick brush and fog. And for one second I could've sworn I saw a girl hiding behind a tree, watching.

"Hey, did you see—" I pointed but there was nothing there.

"Jack the Ripper *was never found!*" Baz said. He fell on me like Bela Lugosi, and I had to kick him to make him stop.

Fifteen miles over a bridge and up a mountain in the back of a horse-drawn wagon made my butt feel like it was made of beef jerky and pain. Finally, the forest thinned out a bit. I could see sunbaked red roofs and thin ribbons of smoke spiraling from crooked chimneys. A stone perimeter like the ones we'd seen on our way blocked off the village from the forest. The same white powder was there. The driver stopped short of the stones, keeping his horse well away from them. The fee was paid. John wasn't happy about having to part with more of his grandparents' money.

"You know, this wasn't even my idea," he grumbled.

"Quit yer bitchin'," Baz said. "What else are you gonna spend it on?"

"Porn," Isabel said with a snort. "I hear after one hundred site memberships, you get one free."

Baz staggered back, his hand over his heart. "Oh! You've been owned by the 'bel, Johnster!"

"Shut up," John said, and swatted Baz's arm harder than he needed to.

To our right stood a tall pole with a bell and a rope. The driver clanged it, and a few minutes later an old woman in a long pale skirt, long-sleeved brown shirt, and her hair buried under a kerchief came bustling out. She and the driver exchanged a few words, some of them pretty heated. She took a good long look at us: four dirty teenagers who smelled like old sweat and the inside of a train car. When she got to Isabel, she seemed to bristle.

Isabel crossed her arms over her cut-up Ramones T. "Great," she muttered. "Racists. My favorite."

The woman reached into her apron and threw a handful of white powder at us.

Isabel flinched and balled her fingers into fists. "What the hell?"

"Salt," John said, holding her back. Some had gotten in his mouth. "It's salt."

The old woman threw another handful of salt behind

us. "Protection," she said. It was one of two English words she knew, we discovered later. The other was "devil."

She tore off a piece of bread and held it out like she was trying to lure an animal. I guessed we were supposed to take it from her, but when I tried, she stepped away, still holding the bread with a wary expression. The wind picked up with sudden force, pushing us back a little. It whistled through the trees like prayers for the dead. The woman looked worried. I stepped over the stones; the others followed. The wind died down, and the forest was quiet. The old woman dropped the bread back into her apron pocket and wiped her hands on her skirt with a look that said she'd like to wipe us away as easily. Then she turned and stalked away.

"That was weird," Isabel said.

"Yeah. And what was with the bread?" Baz asked.

"Bread is for the living," a voice answered. We turned to see a girl about our age, maybe a little older, sweeping the street. She had dark eyes and long, wheat-colored hair and wore jeans and a Flaming Lips T-shirt. A woman about my mom's age was also sweeping. She wore the same drab, peasant-like clothing as the woman who'd thrown the salt at us. She didn't look up.

"So what? The dead are low-carbing it?" I asked, smiling.

Thankfully, the girl returned my smile. "The dead don't eat. If they did, we'd be even poorer."

"She's hot," Baz whispered. "I could totally see her

doing a spread in a Hot Girls of Necuratul calendar, maybe with a Vlad the Impaler bikini—oof!"

Isabel had elbowed Baz sharply in the stomach.

"Harsh, Iz." He coughed.

"Evolve, Baz," she spat back.

"You speak English," John said to the girl, stating the obvious.

"Yes. I go to university. I'm home for the summer. For the festival. By tonight the tavern will be full of drunkards."

John smiled. "Works for me."

"What is the language anyway?" Baz asked, trying to come off as worldly. "Sounds a little Romanian? Hungarian?"

"It's Necuratuli. It's traditional to the village. Don't bother trying to find a translation. It's too obscure. I'm Mariana, by the way." She stuck out her hand and I shook it, which made the older woman shake her head and mutter under her breath. She spat three times. Mariana rolled her eyes. "My mother. She doesn't believe in anything new and sinful like women shaking hands with men." Mariana answered her mother in Necuratuli, and the older woman gave us another suspicious glare before marching off.

"Don't mind her. She gets nervous about outsiders and new things. So. You are here for the festival?"

"Yeah. We read about it in here." I held up our book. "You know, the whole goat's head, sacrificing lambs, possible pact with the Big D thing."

Mariana laughed. "This is how we get our tourists. Florence has the David; we have Satan. I'm sorry to disappoint you—mostly there are sheep and superstitions. But the wine is fantastic and the festival is a lot of fun. Here. Leave your bags. They'll be safe. That's one of the great things about this town—everything's safe; you never have to worry. Can you imagine doing that in London or New York or Moscow?"

"I got my bike stolen once, and it was locked up," Baz said. He gave her his pretend shy face, and Izzie rolled her eyes. "I really missed the bell the most."

Mariana was a good sport and laughed at his lame, player joke. "So sorry about that. Maybe a little tour of Necuratul will cheer you up. Come on. I'll show you around."

"What's with the stones and salt?" I asked, dropping my pack.

"An old folk custom. Supposed to keep evil spirits out. Nothing undead can cross the threshold. And nothing undead can eat. That's why she offered you the bread while you were still on the other side—to prove you were among the living. If you'd tried to grab the bread while crossing the threshold, you would have been burned to ash."

Baz whistled. "Yowza."

"You get a lot of undead coming in, snapping pictures, asking for I Partied with the Goat's Head T-shirts?" I asked.

Mariana nodded gravely and sighed. "Why do you think they call them unquiet spirits? They trash the rooms at the inn and they don't tip. Anyway, you're not supposed to go into the forest. And you're especially not supposed to take bread into the forest. It's like feeding the undead, giving them power."

"Superstitions, man. Culture of fear. Totally bassack-ward, right?" John smirked.

"Every place has its traditions," Mariana said a little coldly.

Baz leaned in close to his cousin. "Way to endear yourself to the locals, my friend." To Mariana he said, "I love hearing about customs!" He fell in next to Mariana as she led us through the heart of Necuratul.

The guidebook hadn't lied: the town was storybook charming—in a "we fear for our lives" sort of way. Each house was circled with salt. Braids of garlic hung from the windows and were nailed over the doors. Behind the village was a cleared area of rolling farmland pop-ulated by sheep. It was peaceful. Postcard pretty. Then I noticed the scarecrows with the big evil-eye symbols painted over their foreheads. Nobody wants that in the family photo album. But the masterpiece of the whole place was the enormous Gothic church that sat at the top of a hill at the very edge of the town, practically up against the first line of trees. I counted thirteen twisty spires. The entrance was guarded by big wooden doors with faces carved into them. Up close the faces were gruesome. Screaming mouths. Eyes opened wide in terror. People begging—for what, I couldn't say and didn't want to know.

"Wow. Charming," I said.

"I know. Fear is no way to live." Mariana pushed open the doors and we went inside.

"Whoa," Baz gasped.

From the outside there was no way to tell how freaking beautiful it was inside. The walls—every single bit of them—shimmered with colorful, gold-leaf murals. They'd been pretty amazingly preserved.

"This was all done in the Middle Ages," Mariana said. "It is a history of the town."

On the left the panels were like something out of a horror movie. Freaky images of dying crops. Diseased, half-skeletal people covered in sores. Children crying. Dogs attacking each other over a scrap of meat. Dead bodies laid out on carts and set on fire, women weeping nearby. On the right the murals showed a happier story than on the left. Farmers working in their fields. Women baking bread. The crops thriving. Animals grazing peacefully. It looked pretty much like the village we'd just toured, except for one weird thing you had to sort of squint to see. In all the pictures on the right there were shadowy images of children and teenagers in the forest, watching.

"Even the ceiling's painted," John said, craning his neck.

Overhead was just one image. It showed a lake surrounded by forest. The villagers stood in one clump
beside it. The children stood in the lake up to their waists.
Their hands were tied together with rope. A priest in a
red, hooded robe held aloft a goat's head that seemed to
have braids coming down from its horns. It was creepy
but also kind of funny. Heidi the Goat's Head of Satan.
Actually, I'd seen girls in the clubs sporting a look pretty
similar to that. A thick mist was coming over the trees,
and the children had their faces craned toward it while
the adults kept their eyes on the goat's head. The water
around the children bubbled and swirled.

"That's a happy picture," I cracked.

Mariana shivered. "So bizarre, isn't it?" She laughed.
"You didn't have to grow up staring at that thing. Believe
me, it kept us all in line."

I was glad for the joke. The church really did give me
the creeps.

"So what's with the Heidi braids on the goat?" I
asked.

Mariana walked to the altar where a huge book was
propped. She flipped pages until she got to a drawing
that showed the goat's head up close and personal: the
glowing eyes, the braids pooled under its chin. But in
this drawing, it was clear that the braids were made up
of lots of different kinds and colors of hair.

Isabel recoiled. "What. The. Hell?"

"The Soul of Necuratul," Mariana explained.

"According to the story, during the dark time, every seven years, each family sacrificed one child to Satan in exchange for security. To show that you were loyal, that you would keep your promise and follow through, you had to cut the child's hair and twine it into a plait attached to the goat. By doing that you promised your child's soul."

"That is seriously f'ed up, man," Baz said staring at the picture.

"But they believed it was necessary. And beliefs have power. That's why superstitions are so hard to root out," Mariana said. She ran a finger around the ancient edges of the page. "They say that up until the English missionaries came in the late eighteen hundreds, the sacrifices were still going on."

"Whoa," John said.

"Sorry to scare you," Mariana said with a half-hearted laugh. She closed the book with a heavy *thwump* that sent dust motes spiraling. "Of course, the missionaries put a stop to it right away, destroyed the goat's head, all the symbols, and the red robes—in fact, to this day, the color red is forbidden in this town. It's supposed to be the devil's color. The missionaries started making sure the children were educated and sent some of the boys away to school in England."

"Boys. Figures," Isabel harrumphed.

"Where does that go?" I asked, pointing to an ornate wall at the front of the church. It was painted with golden saints and angels. In the center was another set of carved doors.

"It's called the iconostasis," Mariana said. "It conceals the altar from the commoners, basically. The priest can choose to open the door during mass and let people see the altar or not."

"Can we see?" John asked.

"Sure." Mariana tried the door, frowned. "Weird. It's locked." She held her palms up. "Sorry."

"That's okay," Baz said, standing a little closer to her. "So are they really going to build a power plant here?"

"Next year. That's what they say. That's why all of us made sure to come home for the festival this year. Next year this might all be gone." Mariana looked around sadly for a moment, then seemed to shake off the gloom. "Okay. Now that you've seen the worst of us, come see the best. The lamb stew at the tavern is amazing. The wine's even better. And you don't have to be twenty-one."

"Now you're talking," John said.

When we got to the tavern, there were signs of life. People who did not need AARP cards were arriving. Mariana greeted them like cousins—a lot of them were cousins—and explained they'd returned from their jobs in the cities or schools to participate in the festival. There were younger kids too. They were kicking a make-shift soccer ball around and laughing, which made me a little homesick. A dark-haired guy in a leather jacket kissed Mariana on both cheeks and introduced himself to us. His name was Vasul, and he had a scholarship to the London School of Economics. He was twenty, like Mariana, and looked like a Russian prince. They treated us like old friends. The wine flowed freely. We stayed up until the wee hours of the morning debating life, politics, traditions, modernization. These were the kinds of conversations I figured we'd be having in college, a preview of coming attractions, and I felt like I'd finally arrived. Like I wasn't a kid anymore.

"Watch Uncle Radu. He's getting out the accordion." Vasul snickered.

Mariana buried her face in his shoulder, stifling a laugh.

"What is it?" John asked.

"Just wait," they both said at the same time, snorting.

Uncle Radu, who was about one hundred and two if he was a day, started playing then. I use the word *playing* lightly. It was more like he was skinning the accordion, because the sound it made was the sound of an instrument in pain. Mariana and Vasul lost it, hands over their mouths, their eyes watering. Mariana's mother flashed her a disgusted look. But Uncle Radu kept playing. Another man picked up his violin, and one of the women started singing. The tavern keeper walked around the tables clapping his hands, but the kids joined only half-heartedly, and when that song was over and the next one started, they lost interest and went back to drinking, playing quarters, and having arguments about alternative bands and indie films.

"I'll hear about this later," Mariana whined.

"When my grandmother saw my clothes, she clucked her tongue and walked away," one of the girls at the end of the table said.

The guy next to her stubbed out his cigarette. "There are moments when my parents stare like they don't know what to make of me. Like they're a little disgusted, a little afraid."

Mariana cut in. "Every generation fears the one that comes after. Our music, our clothes, our aspirations. Our youth. It's like they know we will do what they can't anymore."

"Sometimes my aunties will speak in Creole when they don't want us to know what they're talking about. It's like they're messing with us on purpose," Isabel said. "Makes me mad crazy."

Vasul laughed. "Mad crazy," he imitated, and Isabel broke into her most smitten grin. John knotted his fingers with hers and gave them a kiss to make his claim clear.

"I've been home just a few hours and already my parents are asking when I'm going to settle down and give them grandchildren," a girl named Dovka complained. "I'm twenty-one! I have a DJ gig at a club in Bucharest!" She turned to John. "Don't you hate it when they do that?"

"My parents don't really give a shit as long as my grades are good and I don't get arrested. They just give me money so I'll go away and stop interfering with their golf games and Pilates sessions," John said with a bitter laugh, and I felt kind of bad for him. It was like his parents woke up one day totally surprised to discover they had kids, so they just hired a fleet of people to take care of them.

"What about you, Poe?" Mariana asked.

I shrugged. "My parents are okay. Annoying but good-hearted. I don't think they're afraid of me. The state of my room, maybe," I joked. "Mom's from Wisconsin. She talks funny and loves the Green Bay Packers. My dad's a professor, plays too much Tetris when he should be grading papers, collects vintage Stax LPs. My grandmother still holds on to the old ways some."

When I was little, my grandmother used to tell me about being in the internment camps during World War II. And when it was too much for her to talk about, she'd just end the conversation with, "Fear leads to foolishness." Then she'd teach me Japanese calligraphy, guiding my brush gracefully over the paper. Later we'd go to McDonald's. She loved their fries.

Dovka propped her head up with her hand. Her eyes were glassy. "Traditions are nice, though. They bind you together, remind you where you're from."

"Or keep you back." I don't know why I said it. I think I just wanted to take the opposing view.

"Exactly," Baz slurred. His eyes were at half-mast. "Like last year, when I was dating Chloe? My parents got all bunged. And they're, like, total liberals and everything, but they were freaked that she wasn't Jewish. Like all of a sudden the menorah came out and my dad started asking if I wanted to go to temple Friday night." He grinned. "I told him Friday was a different religious occasion: *Doctor Who*. Hey, it's not my fault they don't have TiVo yet."

Mariana gave a thumbs-up. "TiVo!"

"TiVo." Vasul nodded.

Everybody clinked glasses, shouting "TiVo!" till the old-timers shushed us.

"Still," Vasul said when we'd quieted down again. "There are times when I think maybe it wouldn't be so bad to come back here. It's peaceful. It's safe. No STDs, processed foods, pollution." He paused. "No bombs."

Mariana put her hand on his arm. "Vasul survived the terrorism in London. He was at Russell Square. He saw what happened," Mariana explained.

"It could have been me on that bus," Vasul said softly. "Feels like the world's going to hell sometimes. Like nowhere is safe anymore. Except Necuratul."

Everyone raised their glasses in a respectful, quiet toast. "Necuratul."

Mariana said something to Vasul in their language. "Anyway," she said with a sigh, "it's a moot point. These people—our parents and grandparents, great-grandparents—they're getting old now. When they die off, the village will die with them. All this culture will be lost. Especially if they're relocated because of the power plant. I've seen it happen before. Diaspora."

"That's sad," Isabel said softly, and I knew she was thinking about her own family forced out of Haiti and transplanted in American suburbs where they never quite got past the polite smiles of their white neighbors.

"Shit happens." Dovka grunted. "Get over it. On with the new."

Mariana rolled her eyes. "You're right. This is getting morbid. I don't want to get morbid. I want more wine." She poured us all another round and raised her glass for the third time. "An offering to the future."

"An offering to the future," we all seconded, well on our way to getting completely plastered.

In the corner the older villagers eyed us warily, like we were something to be watched, something that might explode and take them out with us. They continued with their music, singing and playing in controlled measures. But our table started up with The Clash's "Should I Stay or Should I Go," giggling over the implications. We were younger and louder, and soon our voices drowned out the haunting folk song altogether.

The next day it rained like crazy. I'd never seen the sky throw down like that ever. It was a good thing Necuratul was on a mountain because I was sure we'd be flooded otherwise. Mariana, Vasul, Dovka, and the other people our age had left before dawn to get supplies for the festival. That was their job and they did it, hungover or not. Now, with the rain, it looked like they'd have trouble getting back.

"Bridge," the tavern keeper explained in broken English. He made a whistling sound and gestured with his hands: *gone*. Without the others around the villagers weren't overly friendly to us. Actually, I got the feeling they wanted us as gone as the bridge. Mariana's mother ran the bakery. I popped in to buy some bread, which mostly consisted of my pointing and smiling and then laying down money for her to figure out. While she poked through my coins, I looked around the cozy shop. Two burly men sat at a heavy wooden table by the front window drinking steaming mugs of something dark. They stared outright. One guy said something to the other, and they both laughed.

"Just like the seventh grade cafeteria," I muttered to myself, feeling my face grow warm. I kept my eyes forward, taking in the shelves of fresh bread, the plaster walls decorated with evil eyes and garlic, the arched doorway giving a glimpse of the ovens. Something pricked at me. I thought I saw a patch of red inside a partially closed closet. I squinted and suddenly Mariana's mother was closing the door securely. She gave me a tense smile and flicked her gaze at my change. With mumbled thanks I was out the door with my bread, wondering if I'd really seen the forbidden color or not.

I was hustling back to the inn through the downpour when I saw the girl in the forest again. This time she stood, palms out. She was pale, with deep shadows around her eyes, and slime all over her long skirts, like she'd skidded down a hill or something.

"Hello?" I called. "Are you okay?"

She didn't answer, so I moved closer. I was right against the edge of the stone circle. "Do you need help?" I asked slowly, like an idiot, thinking that would help with the language barrier.

She pointed to my loaf of bread.

"You want . . . this? Are you hungry?"

She opened her mouth like a scream, and the trees shook with a thousand whispers that made my neck hair rise. I felt a hand gripping my arm. It was the old woman who had let us in at the gate. Her expression was angry, and she unleashed a torrent of language, all guttural vowels and unfamiliar consonants that made me dizzy.

"I don't understand!" I shouted over the rain.

"Devil," she said, using her only other English word. She flicked her glance toward the forest. No one was there. But I knew I'd seen that girl.

The church bell tolled loudly. In a few seconds many of the villagers, including the tavern keeper, Mariana's mother, and the two men who had been sitting in the bakery, bustled up the hill to the church. They gave me wary glances on the way. None of the children were with them.

"Where did she go?" I asked the old woman. "The girl. Did you see her?"

"Devil," she said again, and hurried to the church with the others. She opened the door, and out of the corner of my eye, I saw that flash of red again. *Red robe*, my brain said. But it was fast, and I couldn't be sure. I couldn't be sure of anything except that I wished Mariana, Vasul, and the rest would hurry back. The old-timers gave me the creeps.

When I got back to the room, I was soaked to the skin, the loaf of bread was inedible, and the others were lying around on the beds and chairs staring off into space. None of our cell phones could get reception here, and it's not like there was an Internet café within a hundred miles. After a full day trapped in our room without so much as a YouTube video to break things up, we were approaching lethal boredom.

"I'm having Internet withdrawal," John said. He was splayed out on the bed balancing the evil-eye pendant he'd bought at the train station on his nose. "Like, seriously, if I can't log on and IM someone—anyone—I'll go insane."

Isabel took out her phone and pretended to text him. "J, OMG, where T F R U?" she chirped in text-speak.

"N hell," John answered back, his thumbs moving in the air. "U?"

"Hell 4 sure. Want BK fries. No garlic."

John laughed, then stopped. "I mean, ROTFLMAO."

I told them about my weird encounter with the girl in the forest and how I'd seen her twice now. I told them about how the old woman who guarded the gate had referred to the forest as "devil."

"I think we should do a creepy field trip to the forest," John said.

The others were on it immediately.

"You guys, what if there are, like, bear traps and poisonous snakes or malevolent, human-flesh-eating reindeer in the forest? Or worse? We could stumble onto a Jonas Brothers appreciation festival." I shuddered for effect.

"Or Beelzebub," Baz said. "The dark lord having a kegger."

"I think we should stay put," I answered.

With a sigh Isabel picked up her phone and pretended to text John. "OMG, J. So f'ing bored. BTW, Poe sux." She glanced at me.

John moved his fingers very deliberately. "Word."

I couldn't take it anymore. I was as pent up and fourteenth-century cabin-crazed as the rest of them. "All right. Creepy field trip. Tomorrow we go to the forest."

The three of them threw their arms around me, and we collapsed on one of the beds, chanting, "Cree-py field trip! Cree-py field trip! Cree-py field trip!"

There was a loud crack, and I was afraid we'd broken the ugly bed. "Dude," John said, holding the shards of his now broken evil-eye pendant. "I'm a marked man." Then he laughed.

The next morning, when the rain had died down to a light patter, we grabbed our flashlights and some fresh bread in case we got hungry.

"Should we take this?" Isabel asked. "I thought that was forbidden."

"You don't go on a trip without food. Didn't you read about the Donner Party?" Baz joked.

Isabel looked uncomfortable. "Still . . ."

"You actually believe that shit?" John kissed her cheek. "Superstition."

"Right. Superstition." Isabel brightened, and we set off for the forest. In one of the narrow lanes between the houses a bunch of kids were playing some kind of game. Five of the kids stood in the center, and the other kids surrounded them. The kids in the outer circle joined hands and went around and around, singing. When they saw us, they stopped and stared.

"Hi." Isabel waved as we passed. They fell in behind us. When we'd turn around, they'd duck behind whatever was available. We could hear them giggling, like following us was the most fun they'd had in a long time. It probably was, but it was making our escape into the forest pretty tricky.

"We're just going for a walk," I explained nervously. "Okay. Bye now. Have fun."

"They're still following us," Baz whispered.

"Stop and do something boring." We stood and gazed at the church. Isabel snapped a few pictures. We talked about architecture, totally making it up. A few minutes later the kids lost interest and ducked down another lane to play something else.

"They're gone," John said. "Let's go for it."

We hurried to the church, creeping around the side. I couldn't see through the stained-glass windows, but I could hear sounds—not quite singing, not quite praying. More like chanting, maybe. Or maybe it *was* praying. It was hard to tell. Isabel motioned for me to hurry up, and I ran to the wall.

John stepped right over the wall and the salt ring. He was on the forest side now. "That's one small step for man, one giant leap for evolution."

"Here goes," Baz said. He and Isabel followed John.

When I got ready to go, I heard those whispering voices on the wind again. "Do you hear that?" I asked.

"Hear what?" Baz asked.

I could almost make out words. One sounded like "avenge," but I couldn't be sure.

"Nothing," I said. "Let's go."

As a joke Baz dropped the bread crumbs behind us, Hansel and Gretel style. "So we can find our way back—*if* we come back. Mwahahaha!"

Isabel rolled her eyes. "Shut up."

The forest itself was pretty amazing: lush and green with the most fantastic black-spotted mushrooms growing wild everywhere. The only weird thing was there were no animals. No deer. No birds. Nothing with a pulse except us.

John and Isabel continued an argument they'd started a few weeks back. I didn't even think they cared about what they were saying anymore, but neither wanted to concede.

"I just think everybody in America should speak English. I mean, if I moved to France, I'd learn French, right?"

"No you wouldn't," Isabel said, laughing. It was her you-are-beneath-me laugh. "You'd hire someone to speak French for you, John."

"You think I'd outsource my language?" he taunted.

"In a heartbeat."

"You know, Isabel, it's not my fault I'm not poor," John teased, but there was something a little mean in it. "It's like you want me to apologize for having money until it comes in handy. No offense, but you know you guys wouldn't even be here right now without me."

Isabel pointed a finger. "There it is: the entitled attitude. One minute you're all, 'Oh, don't blame me; I'm not elitist,' and the next you're like, 'Don't forget I have more money and therefore more say than you do!'" She was breathing hard.

"God! You just . . . twist around everything I say."

"No! I'm just saying what you really feel! Sometimes I think you're only dating me so you can say you've dated a black girl."

John looked hurt. "Take that back."

"Why? It's true, isn't it?"

"Guys, could we give it a rest?" I said. A fog was rising. It made the landscape gray and indistinguishable, and I needed to get my bearings.

Isabel tried not to look wounded, but I knew her too well. "Stop enabling them, Poe. They'll never let us into the club on their own. You just want to think they will."

"Hey," Baz held out his arms. "What am I, chopped liver? Like my people weren't also enslaved and persecuted? Like we didn't get slaughtered in places just like this one?"

"Prejudice isn't the same thing as racism," Isabel argued.

"Yeah? Six million dead might disagree with you there, Iz."

"I'm not the bad guy, Iz," John said softly.

Those weird whispering voices were swirling through the trees again, making my ears hurt. "Guys . . ."

There was a sound off to my right. A branch breaking. A face peeked out from behind a tree. It was the girl I'd seen on the way in. She didn't look very old, maybe seven or eight. Her hair was wet, but her skirts and blouse were caked in grime and mud, like she'd been swimming in a filthy lake. She called out to us in a foreign language.

"Sorry," I said. "We don't speak . . ."

She opened her hand to show us the bread crumbs there.

"Holy . . ." Quickly I glanced behind us. No crumbs. She'd obviously been following us from the beginning. Suddenly I felt disoriented and unsure of the way back. Just then she hitched up her skirts and started running into the forest. Without thinking I ran after her. "Don't let her get away!" I yelled.

She dodged under low-lying branches that smacked me in the face and sprinted easily around every obstacle. She knew the way and had the advantage, but we still managed to keep her in our sights. Deep down I knew we were headed farther into the forest. We reached a part where the fog was even thicker, and the trees were dead and gray, like they'd survived a fire and never grown back. The ground was no longer cushioned by leaves and vegetation. It was stony and scarred, scabbed.

"Don't lose her!" I yelled to the others.

"This fog is intense!" Baz yelled back. "I couldn't find my own ass in this soup."

"You can't find your own ass most days," Isabel shot back. She was keeping pace with me.

The fog thinned slightly. The girl stood beside a wide, deep lake surrounded by more of those dead trees. It was weird because everywhere else the forest was lush and colorful. But this spot was barren. Like nothing had ever grown here. Like nothing ever would. It was colder too—more like October than August. About ten feet out the rounded tops of polished stones showed just under the water.

The little girl looked out at the lake and then moved on to a cave. She whistled, and soon more kids stepped out. I counted them—five, six, ten. They were pale and half-starved looking, all in peasant-style clothing wet with algae and dirt, like they'd been out here for a while. One, a boy of about sixteen maybe, walked over to us. I didn't know whether to run or stay put. Hadn't the villagers told us not to come to the forest? What if these kids were feral? What if they were killers? Instinctively we closed ranks, hands at the ready in case we needed to fight our way out.

"Hey," I said, forcing a calm into my words I didn't even remotely feel. "We're just out for a walk, okay? We don't mean any harm." To the others I whispered, "Start walking backward."

"Can't," Isabel squeaked. "Look."

The way back was cut off by a pack of about ten more creepy kids.

"We just want to go back to the village," I said.

John pulled out his wallet. "Hey, you guys want money? I got money."

"John, shut up, man," Baz said.

The kids closed in, surrounding us, cutting off any

hope of escape. They smelled earthy and damp, like they were part of the forest. While we watched, they gobbled down the bread crumbs. The little girl who'd led us here offered me a bottle of dark liquid.

"*A bea*," she said. I'd heard that at the tavern. It meant drink. "Vin." I knew that too: wine.

"Dude, don't drink that shit. It could be anything," Baz cautioned.

I shook my head, and three of the older kids grabbed Baz and dragged him toward the lake. Before any of us could do anything, they shoved his face under the water. His long arms thrashed and tried to grab for anything he could, but there were more of them and a mob always beats one—even if that one is six foot four with the strength of a Death Metal drummer, which Baz was. We tried to run for him, but they surrounded us, holding us back.

"Okay! I'll *a bea* the *vin*!" I shouted, reaching for the bottle.

They let Baz up. "Holy fuck!" he managed between coughing fits.

I knew it had been a bad idea to come into the forest. My grandmother used to say you should listen to your instincts. The morning the men came to tear her family from their home in California, she'd woken up at four in the morning with the urge to run. Instead she'd tried to calm herself by arranging her dolls around a teacup, like everything was fine. "That is what we do," she said to me as we waited for the bus. "We try to kill the voice inside that says the truth, because the fear of the truth is greater than any other fear."

The girl brought the bottle to my mouth. "*A bea.*"

My hand was shaking as I took a drink and swallowed. It tasted like cheese gone to mold. I gagged and felt a tide of panic rise inside me.

"Poe!" Isabel grabbed my arm. "You okay?"

"Tastes like shit," I coughed out. But I was okay. No poison seemed to be working its way up my throat. My heart was still beating fast, though. One by one, we were forced to drink from the bottle. It came around three times, and then we were made to sit together under the gray carcass of a tree.

"Now what?" Baz asked. Water dripped down his face still.

The kids stood around us, waiting. For what, I didn't know, and I was afraid to find out. About ten minutes later I started to feel a strange, creepy-crawly sensation under my skin, and the forest seemed to breathe. When the wind whispered past my ears, I could swear I heard it say, "Vengeance."

"Izzie?" I heard myself whisper, but she didn't answer. On a nearby rock I saw a kid drop one of the black-spotted mushrooms into the wineskin.

"What'd you give us?" I slurred. "What the hell's in that?"

"Something to help you see," the girl answered, and I

understood her perfectly.

"I see just fine. Twenty-twenty." But already the corners of my vision were curling up on themselves, revealing whatever lies underneath. I walked through chambers of madness. Each one seemed like the end of a dream, only I'd "wake up" and find myself living inside another dream.

I'm walking down the corridor of a jostling train. Left and right, the compartments are filled with the undead: skeletal faces; hollow, haunted eyes; burned, bruised, mangled bodies. They look up like they're expecting something of me. Mrs. Smith calls from the end of the corridor, "This journey is only just beginning, Poe Yamamoto."

I'm standing in the church with many others. The scene reminds me of the one painted on the ceiling. A priest in a red, hooded robe reads from a giant book. In the center of the room seven kids are gathered together. They don't seem frightened. While the priest reads, one of the women cuts a lock of hair from each child and weaves it into the plaits streaming from the goat's horns, tying it off with string.

Now I'm one of the children. They've taken us to the lake. It's cold and I want to go home to eat lamb. Instead they force us into the lake. The water is freezing and dark. We don't want to go in but they make us. Our hands are tied together. If one struggles, we all struggle and the ropes tighten around our wrists. Children plead. The priest holds the goat's head high, chants some words: *Let our crops be plentiful and good. Seal our borders against our enemies. Accept our sacrifice as a token of our faith in you, Dark Lord.* The mist comes barreling over the lake and under my feet; the bottom of the lake gives way. I'm being sucked down fast.

I'm at the tavern. Inside the closet by the door is a hook. On the hook is a red robe. Scissors cut hair. It falls into a bowl in sheets. The old-timers gather around it, looking. "Devil," the old woman at the gate says to me. "Devil."

I started coming out of my drug-induced hallucinations. "Isabel?" I called. I didn't see the others, so I staggered to my feet, calling for them. "Baz! John!" I was completely alone. The fog danced on the surface of the lake. The stones. They seemed to be swaying. Moving. Rising. They weren't stones at all. They were the heads of children—hundreds of them—rising from the lake where they'd been drowned years, centuries ago. Snakes threaded through their hollow eye sockets. Moss clung to their cheeks. Lips had rotted away, exposing mottled bone and nubs of decayed teeth.

"They mean to make the offering again," they whispered. "A sacrifice to save Necuratul. It has begun. Tomorrow, no one is saved. Avenge us." Their words swirled around me like the rustle of dry leaves. "Avenge us."

The girl I'd seen first, the one who'd led me into the forest, stepped forward. Her skin seemed pixilated. When I looked again, tiny moths covered every part of her. They flew away, and underneath her skin was ice white and crawling. Maggots.

With a shout I startled awake. My friends were passed out next to me by the lake. No stones were visible; only the slightest cloud of fog hovered there. I shook my head in case this was another dream. It was darker now, and I had lost all sense of time. Our loaf of bread was missing, but a new bread-crumb trail had been laid out.

"Get up," I said, nudging my friends awake. They sat with effort and struggled out of their stupors. I told them what I'd dreamed. "I think they—the old-timers in the village—are planning to sacrifice us."

"Where are those kids?" Baz said, looking around.

"Gone," I said. "Just like we need to be."

We followed the crumbs back to the village, pausing at the protective stone wall. We'd been gone a while. Early dusk was settling in. I could see some of the villagers in the lanes, sweeping, greeting neighbors, closing up shop, business as usual.

"We can't let them know that we know," I whispered to the others. "We go back to the inn, pack up our stuff, and once it's quiet, we grab our flashlights and head back down to the train station, even if we have to walk all night."

"What about the bridge?" Baz asked.

"We don't know if they're telling us the truth or not. We'll deal with that when we get there."

Isabel slipped her arm through mine like it was the first day of school all over again. "What about Mariana and Vasul and the others? We should warn them."

"I'm not staying," John said. He looked at Isabel. "Let's get out of here."

My gut said cut and run, but not warning Mariana and Vasul seemed like we might as well be committing murder. "We warn them. Then we run."

We slipped back in by way of the church and stepped out casually, just tourists taking an evening stroll. Everything looked different. Ominous. The lanterns on their hooks. The scarecrows in the fields. The evil-eye pendants dangling in the wind. The stars twinkling into early-evening existence. Nothing felt right anymore.

The old woman who'd let us in, the town's gate-keeper, was making her nightly rounds. When she got to the wall, though, she dropped her box of salt and started squawking, crying. The protective ring was completely gone, and in its place was a thin strip of charred earth. Vasul came running over, his traveling bag still on his shoulder. He soothed her until she calmed down.

"What happened?" I asked, but I didn't look him in the eye.

"She thinks it's a sign the seal has been breached and the vengeful spirits of the dead can enter." He shook his head. "I told her it was the rain and the ground was corroded by all that salt. I told her not to worry."

"Yeah, I'm sure that's it," Baz said, his sarcasm barely concealing his fear.

"What's wrong?" Vasul asked.

"What if she should worry?" This time I did look him in the eyes. "What if there's something out there?"

Vasul raised an eyebrow. "Don't tell me you're starting to catch the village superstition."

"No," I lied.

"Good. Because tomorrow's festival is going to be fantastic! You should see everything Mariana and I brought back. We, my American friend, are going to feast till we puke."

I shoved my hands in my pockets. "Actually, um, we're not gonna be able to make the festival. We have to leave a day early if we want to see Prague before we head back to the states."

Vasul crossed his arms and smirked, and I felt like the biggest chickenshit in the world. "So . . . you're telling me you took a fifteen-hour train ride from Munich followed by another fifteen miles of torture-by-wagon up the mountain just so you could come to the festival and tell all your friends back home about it, and now you're not even going to stay to see it?"

In my mind I could see those dead kids rising from the lake. I could see the girl's body turning to maggots.

"Vasul," I started, hoping I could finish. "What if

the sacrifices to Satan . . . what if they're starting them again?"

He nodded mock seriously. "Riiiight."

"It's true!" Isabel said. "They're up to something."

Vasul laughed, but when he saw how scared we all looked, his smile faltered and was replaced by a hurt expression. "You know, I've seen real evil. Bodies lying in the streets. Mangled steel. Bombs exploding." He shook his head like he was trying to clear our words from it. "But these people? They are old and harmless and on their way to being obsolete. They're not doing anything except what they've always done: farm, make bread, have families. They cannot even stop a power plant from taking over their village. I thought better of you people."

What he said made me feel like a Grade A jerk. But what about what had happened to us in the forest? What we'd seen?

"Dude, we need to tell—" Baz started.

"Hey, there you are!" Mariana walked across the square smiling. She looked different. "They're roasting the lamb. It smells wonderful in there. I can't wait to—"

"You got a haircut," I said suddenly.

"Yeah." She turned around, modeling it. "My mother did it for me. She insisted, actually. Said it was too long for my face. Mothers," she said, rolling her eyes. "What do you think?"

In my mind I could see only that awful braid attached

to the goat's head. "Your mother . . . cut your hair," I repeated numbly.

"Yes. I mean, it's not a fancy salon in Paris, but I can't afford that anyway, and she's pretty good with the scissors if you sit straight and don't fidget."

They had Mariana's hair.

"My grandmother gave me a little trim this morning too." Vasul ran his hand across the top of his head. "Want to be at our best for the festival, you know."

Hadn't I seen the old-timers rushing to the church? Hadn't I seen a red robe?

One of the younger kids, a chubby-cheeked boy, ran up to Mariana and said something. She stroked his head and cooed an answer. The boy gave us a quick look and smiled before running back to his pals.

"What was that?" I asked.

"He wanted to know if you would play their game with them. I told him maybe later," Mariana explained. "What's the matter? You seem upset."

"There's something we should tell you," I heard myself say. "Meet us in our room as soon as you can."

A few feet away the kids started up their game again. The outer circle descended on the kids clumped together on the inside. And they all fell down, laughing hard.

Ten minutes later Mariana and Vasul joined us in our room at the tavern, and Baz quickly bolted the door behind them.

Mariana searched our faces. "What's going on?"

"We went to the forest," I started.

Mariana's eyes widened. "You what? Poe, you shouldn't have done that. You could have been hurt. There are old rusted traps and deep holes and probably rabid bats."

"You forgot ghosts," I said.

Vasul held up his hands. "Not this again."

"Just listen, please," I begged. "What if there really is a reason they don't want you to go into the forest? What if they don't want Necuratul to die? What if they're planning to do something about it, like make another sacrifice?"

Mariana and Vasul exchanged glances.

"What do you mean?" Vasul asked.

I told them everything. The lost children. The visions. The warning.

"I know it sounds crazy, but before I came on this trip, this fortune-teller told me I'd be tested. That this was a test of some kind. What if she was right?"

Baz licked his lips nervously and lowered his voice. "They cut your hair. That was always the first part of the ritual, right? Cut the hair and weave it into a braid to show your intent, your loyalty to Satan."

"Then say the incantation and drown them in the lake," Isabel finished. "Right?"

"Mariana, you said it yourself in the church: superstitions have power. That's why they're hard to root out,"

John added. He was pacing.

"I think they've decided to go back to the old ways," I said. "The really old, bad ways. Today I swear I saw someone wearing a red robe in the church—"

Vasul shook his head. "No one wears red in this village anymore. Not since the old days. It's considered bad luck, like tempting the devil."

"I saw it," I insisted, but now I wasn't so sure. I was accusing Mariana's mother of something awful, and I half hoped I was right so I wasn't crazy, and I half hoped I was wrong because it was a terrible thing to imagine.

"Poe's not the only one. We were all there. Those *kids*—" Isabel stumbled over the word. "Whatever they are—they were warning us!"

Vasul and Mariana huddled together, whispering in their own language. I couldn't read their expressions. Were they frightened? Upset? Angry? Did they even believe me? They hugged, and then Mariana turned back to us. Her eyes were as dark as the evening shadows glooming up the room. "If what you're telling us is true, we have to leave as soon as possible. We have to gather the children . . ."

"I didn't survive the London School of Economics to end up in a lake," Vasul tried to joke, but his smile was a ghost.

"Mariana, did your mother give anybody else haircuts?" I asked.

"All of us. All of the children," she whispered.

"We have to warn the others," Vasul said softly to her.

She looked at him for a long time. "None of the old ones can stay up past eleven, eleven thirty. That's to our advantage. We'll round up the children and take them to the church around midnight. When we're sure it's safe and there are no old ones around, we'll give you the signal: a lantern in the front window. It's going to be quick, so you'd better be looking for it. We can't afford to do it twice. When you see it, haul ass to the church."

"And then what?" John pressed.

Mariana's mouth was set in a grim line. "Then we get the hell out of here."

We tried to act normal. At dinner we sat in the tavern, pushing meat around on our plates with our bread. If the old-timers noticed, they didn't say anything. Then we went up to our room to sit by the window with its view of the church pressed against the ominous forest and waited. The moon rose, a red wound in a dark sky. I'd never seen a moon that color before. It was exactly the kind of sight that we'd hoped to take pictures of and post on our Web pages—AWESOME RED MOON OVER NECURATUL! But right now it just gave me the shivers.

"What time is it?" Isabel asked.

"Midnight," I answered.

"Where's the signal?" Baz peered into the night-hushed town.

"Maybe we should just go," John said. "They know the score."

"We promised," I said, but I honestly wanted to run.

My watch showed five minutes after, then ten. Every passing second seemed a lifetime. Finally white light strobed across the front window of the church, once and out, just like Mariana had said.

"Come on," I said.

We sneaked down the stairs with our shoes in our hands, careful not to make a sound. Dying firelight came from the kitchen. Mariana's mother, the tavern keeper, the old woman at the gate, and several other old-timers sat at the table. Their voices were hushed but urgent, like when your parents are having a fight they don't want you to know about. We held our breath. How could we get past without being seen? I motioned for Izzie to go first. She made it to the door and gently lifted the latch, nudging the door open by degrees. John tiptoed out next, followed by Baz. A little gust of wind banged the door shut after him.

Chairs scooted across the kitchen floor. Mariana's mother and the tavern keeper hurried over, and I sank down and huddled in the shadowed staircase. Satisfied that everything was okay, they headed back to the kitchen and their discussion. Whatever they were talking about, it was full of passion and fervor, and Mariana's mother seemed like she was trying to convince the others of something. I wasn't sticking around for more. Quickly I slipped out after my friends, and we raced to the church through empty streets, the darkened houses like sleeping guards that could come awake at any moment. Up on the hill the church loomed.

The door had been left ajar, so we slipped in. A few prayer candles burned at the back of the church, but their pool of light wasn't very wide. I didn't see anyone.

"Mariana?" I whisper-yelled into the gloom. "Vasul?"

A soft moan came from the front of the church. We followed it. "It's from behind the iconostasis," I said. This time the door opened easily.

"Holy . . ." Baz said. This part of the church was painted too. But it was a different history on these walls. Murders. Hangings. Mob violence. Enemies crucified upside down. The gruesome goat's head—the Soul of Necuratul that was supposed to have been destroyed—had been propped up inside a niche in the wall like a treasured relic. A candle glowed beneath it, casting light up, making the hollow eyes seem alive with a strange fire. The plaits of child's hair fell to the floor and pooled several inches thick.

The moan again. Izzie flicked on her flashlight and swooped it around. The light fell on the altar. Mariana had been tied up and stretched out there. Her mouth was gagged, but she tried to speak anyway. Or scream would be more like it. She was looking at something just behind us.

I never saw the blow coming.

* * *

Above me the ceiling of the church came into focus. Those children cowering in fear in the lake, their parents readying the stones to weigh them down. My head felt like it had skidded along the pavement for a mile.

"Can you hear me?" Mariana's voice.

My head throbbed as I turned it in her direction. Mariana stood a few feet away, a blur of red. I blinked and she came into focus. She wore a hooded red robe.

"It's called devil's cloth," she said as if I had asked a question. "It was worn by the priest who would consecrate the sacrifice to the Dark Lord. Of course, traditionally that priest was male, but we're trying to marry progress with tradition here."

I tried to move and found my hands were bound together and a rope had been slipped around my ankles. It was the same with my friends. All the young people stood around us. None of the old-timers were present. It was an under-twenty-five crowd only. The children had been gathered and brought around. They looked sleepy and curious, like this was some kind of game they were playing but they didn't understand the rules just yet.

"What are you doing?" I croaked.

"Putting things right. Saving Necuratul before it's too late," Mariana answered.

"The old-timers. Did they make you do this? Are they forcing you to—"

They all laughed.

"The old-timers? Force us? They begged us not to do it! Every single one of them was ready to pack up and leave Necuratul, let the bulldozers and 'progress' take it. Be obliterated by people with more power than we have. 'Make do,' they pleaded. 'Appreciate what you have.' But we've seen the world. We know only the powerful are respected and safe." She joined hands with Vasul and Dovka. "So we start the tradition again. But we modernize. Why sacrifice our own when we could sacrifice others?"

Dovka snipped a small section of hair from each of us. "Once we join your hair to the goat's head, your souls will be promised to the other world."

"But that's not fair," Isabel said. "We had no say."

"Life isn't fair," Dovka answered.

John was sweating heavily. "Look, my parents are rich. They'll pay any ransom."

"John, what are you doing, man?" Baz growled.

"S-sorry, cuz," he stammered.

"John," Baz said again, but that was all.

Mariana glanced from John to us and back again. "You would be willing to leave your friends, your own cousin, to their fates?"

John wouldn't look at us. "Don't hurt Isabel."

"John . . ." Isabel started and stopped.

"The breakdown of civilization, the end of the tribe. No loyalty," Vasul said. "This is what the world is."

"At the club where I work, there are so many bored,

rich kids. Totally entitled. Always looking for that next thrill to talk about over beers. Just like this one," Dovka sneered.

"I didn't mean any disrespect," John choked out.

Mariana thought for a minute. "Very well. You can be part of our new tradition."

"Whatever you want. I'll do it."

"I am glad to hear it." She jerked her head, and Dovka drew a razor from her pocket and moved so fast I could barely register what was happening. I hope it was the same for John. Isabel shrieked John's name, and the next thing I knew, John was on the ground, lifeless, and the rest of them were spattered with blood.

"Oh god, oh god, oh god," Baz keened. He closed his eyes and started a prayer in Hebrew, even though I knew he hadn't been to temple since his bar mitzvah. This was the kind of fear that made you pretend there was a god to save you. The kind that brought everything into such sharp relief that you could watch a friend die and still hear a mouse scuttling in the corner, the wind whistling against the side of the church.

Isabel had gone silent.

Mariana put her hand on John's head. "We offer not only our loyalty but this blood as well, O lord, as a promise of our fidelity. From now on we will always make such an offering. It is a new world and that calls for new commitment."

The kids huddled together. They looked scared.

Dovka spoke soothingly to them and they calmed. She had them wind our hair into the braids on the goat's head and they did it without question. Dovka said something in Necuratuli. "To prove our loyalty," she translated, looking at us.

Mariana opened the ancient rites book and began to read in a tongue that demanded attention, a language that spoke to your bones, made your heart beat faster, whispered to all those places inside that hide our worst thoughts, our most terrible fears. It was a calling-up, a calling-out. A naming. When she was finished, she closed the book and forced us to our feet. The kids had finished their grisly task, and Mariana's crew tied Baz, Isabel, and me together. Our hands were fastened to the point of pain. Another rope was tightened around our waists and Dovka held the slack. Vasul and the other guys carried John's body on their shoulders like pallbearers.

Just then the door to the church banged open. The old-timers blocked the exit with their shovels and lanterns. Mariana's mother spoke sharply to her daughter, and Mariana answered in English.

"We won't stop, Baba. This is the future. In the hundred and thirty years since the village stopped the sacrifice, things have only gotten worse. It's time to start again. Our generation will have everything."

The tavern keeper grabbed hold of Mariana's wrist, but she broke his grip easily. "Uncle Sada, you can't stop us. You should thank us, instead. We are saving the village," Mariana insisted.

"You will curse us all," he answered back in English, surprising me.

The old-timers rushed them then, but there weren't enough of them, and they weren't strong enough to stop what was happening. The younger ones held them back easily. "Now we go to the lake," Mariana said.

The group pushed us through the village, the old-timers following, pleading. We left them standing on the other side of the wall. They looked worried, like parents sending their kids off to prom instead of cold-blooded ritualistic murder.

Dovka pulled us after her into the forest. If we slowed, she gave the rope around our waists a sharp tug, and we'd stumble into one another. Fighting back was out of the question. The night was warm and oppressive. It pushed its hands against our lungs, made us sweat as we trudged through the forest in a clump. Somebody started singing. The Stones. "Sympathy for the Devil."

"Pleased to meet you, hope you guess my name . . ."

There were a few giggles, like this was a fraternity prank, a bunch of kids on their way to outsmart their friends in some goofy one-upmanship. I even tried to tell myself that—anything to rationalize what was happening. But then I'd remember the razor at John's throat, and the terror would come over me again. The singing got louder, and Vasul shushed them. John's lifeless body was slung over Vasul's shoulder. We carried on in silence, the lanterns lighting the way. The lake with its top hat of fog came into view. Dovka stuffed our pockets and shirts with heavy stones and pushed us into the cold, black water.

"Go out farther," Mariana called, holding a gun on us. We stumbled backward until only our heads were visible. "That's good. Now we wait."

"I'll n-never sit in the student union studying," Isabel stammered through tears. "Never go to a frat party or date an Irish boy named Declan."

"Guys named Declan are all assholes," I tried to joke, but it came out hollow.

Baz had stopped praying. In the four years we'd been friends, he'd never been so quiet, so still.

Vasul and his friends laid John's body on the ground.

"Why are we waiting?" one of the guys asked. "Let's get this done."

"We've made the offering. It's up to The One to accept it," Mariana said with finality.

In the distance I could hear the old-timers singing the old songs, skeletal melodies with nothing to disguise the despair. Dirges. My grandmother said that when her father had succumbed to the dysentery in the camp, her mother sang until her voice was ragged. Like that was the only thing left to her.

The night pressed on. The cold water numbed us, and Isabel's teeth chattered. I tried to move my fingers just to keep the circulation going, anything to keep from losing feeling or falling asleep and going under. At first, I counted silently, trying to keep my mind from going to dark places, but when I reached two thousand eighty-three, I couldn't remember what came next, and that scared me so bad I stopped.

After a while Dovka got bored and started a conversation about remixes. Somebody chewed gum, offered the pack to the others. A girl slapped at a bug on her arm, flicked it off. It was all so ordinary. Just a to-do list that included murder. And I wondered what had happened, what flipped that switch in the human brain that allowed people to rationalize atrocities, whether it was racism or terrorism or genocide or drowning people you'd shared wine with, their pockets heavy with stones you picked up yourself and put there.

Under the water I felt Isabel grasping my hand, and I was glad for the feel of it. Seemed the only thing I could be sure of right now. "S-sorry I p-put that Celine Dion ringtone on your phone that time," she said.

"That was you?"

"Yeah."

"You suck."

"Yeah." She bit off her laugh when it became a cry.

Suddenly Mariana stood at attention, motioned to the others. "It's happening,"

The fog thickened and there was a strong smell, like sulfur, that made me feel as if I were choking. Bubbles appeared on the surface of the lake, and it was noticeably warmer. Uncomfortable, like a sauna. The mud beneath our feet seemed to give way a bit. Baz was in only neck deep, but Isabel's mouth dropped below the waterline, and I wasn't far behind her. She snapped her head back, trying desperately to keep her nose free, and Baz and I pushed against her as best we could to keep her upright. But it was hard with our hands tied behind our backs. Isabel panicked and nearly brought us down with her thrashing.

"Hold on, Iz," I said, nudging her up with my shoulder. "Don't let her fall, Baz."

In answer he gave her a boost from his side.

The mud gave just a little more, and the water swirled around us. Isabel was crying now and blowing bubbles, coughing out water.

Mariana and the others were like ghosts on the bank silhouetted by ravaged trees. "Necuratul, Necuratul, Necuratul," they chanted. Something was coming through the forest. I heard cracking sounds and the sulfur smell grew stronger. I could barely breathe.

I yelped as something brushed against me in the black water.

"What was that?" Isabel cried out.

The bump came again, pushing us forward this time. I stumbled and Baz yanked on the rope, keeping the three of us upright. The movement was everywhere at once. The wind picked up.

"Vengeance," it whispered.

Something bumped me again. Then we saw the heads rising from the deep, dark lake, the dead eyes circled in shadows, the open mouths where maggots and small snakes crawled. They surged past us to the bank, and the fog shifted again. It was hard to see. The forest echoed with screams. Shouts. It wasn't English, but I didn't need a translation. It was the language of fear.

"C-come on!" I tugged on the rope that tied me to my friends. Our pockets and shirts were still heavy with stones and our limbs nearly frozen from our time in the water. Every step was tough going. We stumbled out of the lake and fell to the ground. Our bodies were too heavy to get far. I reached my fingers out and into Isabel's pocket, pushing past the painful burn of the rope as it dug into my wrist. I only managed to pull out two stones. She tried to do the same for me but couldn't reach. A sharp scream came from somewhere inside the forest, and my breath quickened.

"Go, go, go," Isabel said, almost like she was willing herself forward.

"St-stand up. Toward trees," I stammered. I was too cold to say much else.

We struggled to our feet and lurched toward the forest in a sort of step-hop. The fog was heavy. It gave us some cover, but it also hid whatever was happening inside its murky veil, and that thought had me hopping faster, forcing the others to keep up. A few feet in, we came to one of those sharp, dead trees.

"Lean d-down," I said. I got close enough to use the rough edge of a limb to saw through my ropes around my hands, then I untied my friends.

"Oh God," Isabel said, her eyes huge.

I followed her sightline, and through the haze I saw Mariana's horrified face. Behind her the forest was full of the pale, long-dead children of Necuratul, half-eaten by vegetation and looking for justice. They advanced slowly, the bread crumbs falling from their mouths. They fell on Vasul, devouring him until there was nothing left. Then they turned to Dovka. She screamed and struggled as they dragged her into the lake, and she kept screaming until her mouth was filled with water and she disappeared beneath the murky surface. Mariana tried to run. She was stopped by several ghostly boys who held her tight. The hollow-eyed girl who'd led us into the forest that morning put her hands on either side of Mariana's face. Where her hands touched, Mariana's skin turned the color of putrefied leaves. She couldn't even cry out as the rot spread quickly through her body. The dead girl blew gently, and Mariana's decaying body disintegrated into a pile of wet leaves that were trampled by the feet of the dead.

I could hear screams in the fog and make out the voices of the old-timers. The tavern keeper stood at the edge of the clearing, shouting to the younger kids. They ran to him, and he motioned for us to follow. I reached for Isabel, who grabbed for Baz, and then we were forcing

ourselves to stumble-run, our fear working hard to over-
come the heaviness of our soggy clothes and numbed
legs. With the screams of the others still echoing around
us, we kept our eyes on the hope of his lantern. Pretty
soon the lights of the village were close. The wind picked
up again and I got that prickly feeling on the back of my
neck. The forest glowed with a greenish fog; it thinned,
and I saw that the dead were coming after us.

"The soul," they whispered. "Give us the soul."

The village was in view. The old woman who guarded
the gate was shouting in words we didn't understand and
throwing salt everywhere. The kids ran ahead, and she
pushed them inside the gate. I looked back as behind us
the tavern keeper cried out. He'd slipped and fallen, and
the hollow-eyed ones were almost on him.

"The soul," he gasped out. "Must burn."

"Poe!" Isabel shrieked, pulling me along.

We raced inside the gate and the old woman closed
it with a bang and sealed it with salt. In the forest the
tavern keeper screamed. There was no chance of saving
him.

"Holy shit!" Baz shrieked. The three of us were running with the rest of the villagers for the church. "What
the hell was he saying, Poe?"

"The soul must burn," I repeated.

"The hell does that mean?"

"The goat's head." Isabel gasped. "The Soul of Necuratul."

There were more screams. The salt didn't stop the dead. They'd eaten the bread. They had the power now, and they were coming.

"If we burn it, does this end?" Baz asked.

"Only one way to find out," I said.

Isabel was the fastest. She bounded up the hill to the ancient church and had the door open in track-star time.

"Come on!" she yelled. I could hear the scuttling of those dead things coming through the village, could hear the screams of the old-timers who tried to fight them off without success. We reached the church and fell in along with some of the children. A few of the old-timers hurried after, but the whispering dark was bearing down on them. One of the old men from the bakery cried out as the dead showed their long, gleaming teeth and picked his bones clean. Two of the children struggled up the hill. Baz and I started for them, but we couldn't reach them in time. That was when I thought I might lose it completely. We closed the door and sealed ourselves inside the gloomy church. Just us, a handful of kids, and Mariana's mother against an army of the dead. They banged at the door again and again, and we backed away.

"Cut that shit out right now!" Baz yelled. It would have been funny if we weren't completely terrified.

Mariana's mother opened the door of the iconostasis and came back holding the goat's head, which she handed to me. As we were yelling at her to burn it, she was trying to tell us something but we didn't understand. The kids did, though. They ran around checking candles, and I realized we were all on the same page, at least. Mariana's mother went to help them look, while Baz, Isabel, and I stayed up by the iconostasis. One of the kids let out a shout when he found a lighted candle. The banging got louder, and then there was a terrible crash, and the dead were inside.

The hollow-eyed girl stepped forward. She spoke in both her language and ours. "Give us the Soul. The debt must be canceled."

Mariana's mother shook her head at me, her eyes wide.

"If you burn it, we are damned forever," the dead girl said.

The dead surrounded the living children. Mariana's mother looked from them to the Soul of Necuratul in my hands. She shook her head again, and the message was clear: don't give them anything, no matter what. But that meant giving up on the kids. I'd already seen two kids die and I wasn't watching any more go down.

"Here. You want it, come get it." I held out the goat's head.

"Poe. Don't do it, man," Baz pleaded. "Don't give it to the funky dead people."

"We're a part of that now," Isabel cautioned. "Our hair is in those braids."

"We're part of this no matter what we do," I said. "If they can end this, then let them."

The hollow-eyed girl took the goat's head in both hands. She had us follow her into the iconostasis, where she placed the head on the altar and spoke over it in hushed tones. Color flooded the faces of the dead, and the shadows under their eyes faded. And then, with small, contented sighs, many of them disappeared into thin wisps of smoke.

Suddenly the girl stopped speaking. She seemed afraid. She backed away just as the altar caught fire, and something rose from the flames. It was a huge man, more beautiful than anybody I'd ever seen, man or woman. He had long black hair, skin like marble, and wings like an angel, but his eyes were murky as the lake where we'd nearly been drowned. His lips stretched into a cruel smile; his teeth were sharp. And when I turned my head just slightly, he seemed to have the head of some beast with enormous curled horns on either side.

"The debt is paid!" the hollow-eyed girl insisted.

"The debt is never paid," the angel-beast growled in a voice that felt like thousands of flies crawling across my skin. He towered over us. Flames licked at the golden walls. The murals dripped paint, and I could hear screams inside those paintings. The dead who still remained began to melt like wax, puddling on the floor and running through the church. The girl screamed, and that was enough for me.

"Run," I croaked out. "Go!"

We bolted for the doors and pushed our way out into choking smoke. Every part of Necuratul was burning down. Suddenly the hollow-eyed girl was in front of us. I pulled up short. But she motioned for us to follow, and she led us to the forest. Behind us we could hear the beast shrieking. The fire was at our backs and getting closer, and I was afraid the whole forest would go up, trapping us.

Finally we reached a spot where I could see the bridge below us. It was partially under water but still visible. It was passable. The girl pointed to it.

"I can't go farther," she said.

I didn't know what to say, so I only nodded while Isabel and Baz helped Mariana's mother and the children down the hill.

"Poe!" Isabel yelled from the middle of the bridge.

The hollow-eyed girl stepped closer, and my heart hammered in my chest. Backlit by the flames she looked fragile. She leaned in and kissed me full on the mouth, and something shifted inside me like when I'd drunk the tainted wine.

"You can see what lives in the dark," she said. "Do not forget." Fire engulfed a tree. The sparks landed on my sleeve and I had to rub them out. Isabel and Baz were shouting at me.

"Go," she said. Her body began to shift. Move. Like something trying to break out. Her skin exploded then, and thousands of small moths spiraled up, their wings like faint scars against the blue-orange of the fire, the blood of the moon, and then they were gone. I ran for the bridge, and we all crossed it to safety.

It took us all night and well into the next day to make it back to the train station, where the agent said it was a miracle we'd survived the fire. The entire area around where Necuratul had stood had burned to the ground. Nothing left but blackened stumps of trees and ash. It was so damaged, they didn't even know if they could build the power plant there. That's irony for you.

The station agent draped blankets on our backs and made us cups of strong tea. At one point Mariana's mother came over to me, stared into my eyes for a while, and transferred the evil-eye pendant from her neck to mine. Then she walked away to take care of the children. The station agent didn't ask any questions. He handed the three of us a bundle of tickets and put us on the next train out. And all of them stood on the rickety wooden platform watching our train inch away, like they wanted to be sure every trace of us was gone.

Baz and Isabel slept a lot. Every time I closed my eyes, I saw those dead faces, Mariana turning to rot, and the angel-beast rising above us like a threat of something to come—and I'd wake up gasping. It was night, and I made my way to the café car. I ordered a Danish and some black coffee and sat next to the window to watch the night crawl past.

"I told you the pastry was stale, didn't I?"

Mrs. Smith had settled into the seat next to me. She opened her bag and took out a hunk of cheese, offering me some. I shook my head.

"Now you have seen," she said quietly. "Now you know."

"Yeah? What the hell am I supposed to do about it?"

"What do you think? Stop the fuckers."

I stared at her. "How do I do that?"

"You can't fight evil all at once. That was just a small test. There are bigger ones to come, Poe Yamamoto."

I turned away. "I don't want this."

"Who would?" She snapped her handbag shut and stood to go. "Don't lose my card. That's embossing on there. Not cheap."

"What's going to happen?" I asked, but she was already making her way through the car, singing some song that I could have sworn was AC/DC's "Highway to Hell."

Anyway, I don't know if you're still watching this or not. Maybe you clicked on something else—a clip of a cat caught in a ceiling fan or an interview from Comic-Con. Maybe you think I'm making this up, and there's nothing out there in the dark but what our minds conjure up when we're looking for a thrill.

But if you are still watching this, I want to tell you one last thing: On the train ride back I had a dream. It was me and Baz and Isabel, and that fog had come up really quickly. I couldn't see what was ahead, but I felt like it could see us. And then I saw John. His eyes were black pools. A jagged, half circle of a scar made an angry smile at his throat. And his teeth were sharp as the man-beast's.

"There's so much on the other side," he whispered to me. "Things you can't imagine. There's a lot of evil to bump asses with out there, Poe. You have no idea."

He wasn't kidding.

I'm gonna try to keep this account running, update when I can, so you'll know whatever I know. But right now, I gotta go. Baz and Isabel can't hold that door forever and unless you know something about super-powerful werewolves and can text me right this second, then I'm gonna have to go deal.

Just be looking out, okay? Trust the lizard, my friends. Something's going down. Something big. It's already started.

Be ready.